MINIONS OF MERCURY

MINIONS OF MERCURY

WILLIAM GRAY BEYER

ILLUSTRATED BY

SAMUEL CAHAN

COVER BY

VIRGIL FINLAY

STEEGER BOOKS • 2020

PUBLISHING HISTORY

"Minions of Mercury" originally appeared in the August 31, and September 7, 14, 21 & 28, 1940 issues of *Argosy* magazine (Vol. 301, No. 5–Vol. 302, No. 3). Copyright © 1940 by The Frank A. Munsey Company. Copyright renewed © 1967 and assigned to Steeger Properties, LLC. All rights reserved.

Visit steegerbooks.com for more books like this.

CHAPTER I

THE HEAVENLY VISITOR

AT FIRST, OMEGA was slightly puzzled. Since Omega's intellect was practically all-powerful—since in fact, Omega was in reality nothing *but* intellect, a vast, disembodied and slightly irresponsible brain-wave, bewilderment was an almost unheard-of experience for him. But now he could have sworn... In fact it had only been a short twelve years ago when he had sworn that nothing existed on the American continent anything like the very things he now beheld. Twelve years ago, he had told his friend and protégé Mark, that the Scandinavian peninsula was the best place on the surface of the earth for him, Mark, to establish residence.

He had assured Mark that nowhere in America, or what was left of it, was there a vestige of the civilization Mark had known in the days before his six-thousand-year long sleep, a cat-nap caused by an enterprising twentieth century surgeon's maladroit use of a super-anesthetic. When Mark came to, the largest portion of America's inhabitants were savage nomads, some of them cannibals, and the rest of them lived in a more or less feudal condition in the walled cities which were thinly scattered throughout the continent. Omega had been sincere when he had advised Mark to make his home among the Vikings of Norway.

Omega had always taken an interest—sometimes beneficent, sometimes merely meddlesome—in Earthly developments. As

Luna was his birthplace, it was natural to consider Terra as his real home, now that its satellite was cold and dead.

Yet here, on Earth, something was going on that he had missed—an unforeseen development that bordered on the impossible. Omega thought back to the time when he had visited this place. He remembered distinctly that the city had been in a very low state of social development at the time. It was just another feudal town of the many that had sprung up amid the ruins of the civilized communities of the twenty century. Ruled by an iron-fisted despot, it had been plunged in tyranny and squalor when he had last seen it. It had been one of the

"That's Detroit down there," Omega pointed
out. "After thousands of years it's suddenly
become civilized, and I don't understand it."

worst of the lot, in fact. There had been many others with better government and more enlightened laws. More enlightened, that is, for the times.

Omega did whatever a disembodied intelligence could do in the way of frowning with thoughtful effort.

The solution came when he realized that it had been more than a thousand years since he had been here. Time certainly did fly, he thought, happy in his coinage of a phrase. He remembered the progress, both social and scientific, which had been made in shorter periods during the history of mankind. And while it was apparent that other cities in America had remained at a standstill, it was understandable that one of them hadn't.

THAT DEFINITE progress had taken place was easy to see. Factories had sprung up and were puffing up smoke at a furious rate. Vehicles were moving along the streets, and they weren't

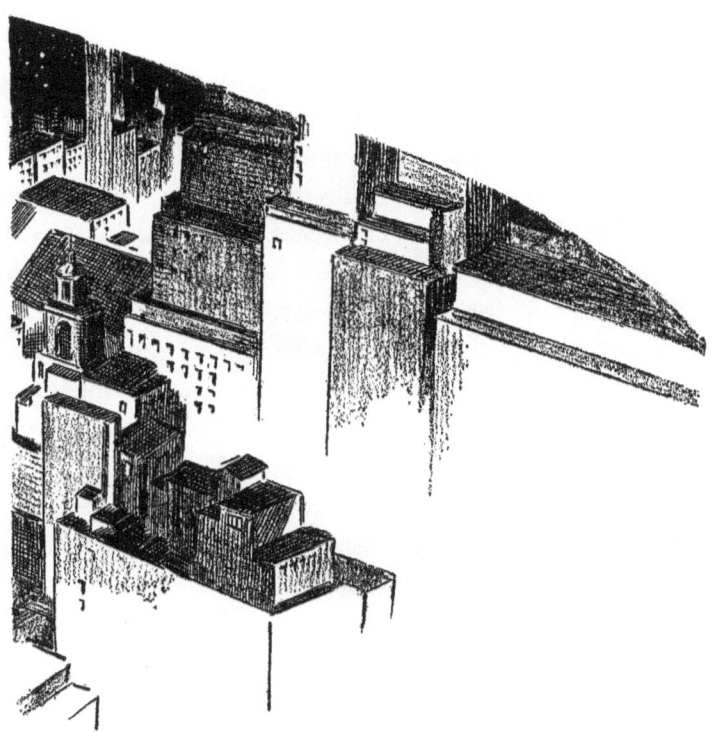

drawn by horses. Idly Omega noted that none of these was traveling in or out of the city, though several wagons pulled by teams of horses were. Yet the roads leading through the gates were smooth and capable of carrying autos.

Further, he noted that most of the horseless vehicles were trucks, designed for freight, rather than passengers. Evidently these people didn't consider that the best use of an automobile was to get them away from the city. No... They wouldn't, naturally. The walls explained that. Outside the city lurked danger, in the form of roving bands of nomads. Though it did seem queer that when some of the inhabitants did venture out, they preferred horsepower to swifter ways of travel. Unless, for some reason, the people of this city didn't want their advancement known to the rest of the world.

Detroit had been the original name of the city below. Possibly that was the reason for the sudden progress. Detroit had once been a great industrial center, chiefly inhabited by those engaged in large-scale manufacture.

It was conceivable that the descendants of these people were slightly different from the inhabitants of other cities. Their ancestors had been skilled workers, technicians and engineers. There was a tendency for such skills to be inherited. Then again, technical treatises and books on science and physics and chemistry might have escaped destruction during the last great war.

These might well have been discovered and deciphered by the descendants of the men and women who had originally used them. And that, no doubt, coupled with natural inherited tendencies, had enabled the new city of Detroit to show such amazing progress since he had last observed it.

With Omega, curiosity was a vice. He decided to investigate. First, he set about whipping himself up a human body to inhabit. He could just as well have descended into the city as the invisible thought-pattern that he was, and thereby have roamed freely about, observing without being seen; but that was not his way.

He preferred to get his information as a man would get it, by mingling with the people he wished to observe. A man can learn more about a man than can all the disembodied intelligences in existence, for the hearts and souls of men cannot be felt and known merely by the processes of the brain.

So Omega created his body—a decrepit and ancient one, with a wrinkled face and wise old eyes—by the direct mental manipulation of the vast energies which pervade all space. Courtesy and discretion caused him to perform the operation at some distance outside the city walls. Then, with tottery steps, he proceeded, with the aid of a cane—literally, an after-thought—toward the nearest gate in the wall.

As he neared it, two men appeared atop the barricade, one on each side of the gate. They were archers; and they were obviously going to make a fuss about letting him in.

"Halt!" cried the hefty one. "Why do you seek entrance?"

"Because I want to be inside, butterball," answered the ancient in a surprisingly hearty voice.

The guards looked at each other, and then the skinny one nodded. As if this was a signal, the other quickly fitted an arrow to his bow and let fly at Omega. The arrow sped true to the mark, in this case, approximately the pit of the aged man's stomach. As it struck, the ringing sound of a gong was heard, and the arrow shivered to bits.

"One cigar," remarked the old one. "How about opening that gate?"

THE ARCHER looked puzzled, then assumed prayerfully that Omega wore some sort of armor under his ragged clothing. Grinning, he reached behind him and produced a high-powered rifle. Omega wondering vaguely why he hadn't used this in the first place, watched the man take careful aim at the central portion of his spurious and non-essential anatomy. This time the sound of the gong and the flat crack of the rifle shot came together. Omega shook his head, grumbling.

"Phooey," Omega said, with dignity. "What manners! You need a lesson, Hawk-Eye." Then he went into action. Taking a short run he made a prodigious leap and landed beside the dumbfounded guard.

"I hate being shot at so early in the morning," growled the ancient. "Give me that!"

The guard, his coarse jaw sagging, handed over the gun, without argument. He had made the fatal but perfectly understandable error of looking into the eyes of the old one; and after that his will was not his own. Omega took a look at the rifle. It resembled a model that had seen wide-usage during the great war which had finally wrecked civilization. Smokeless powder had been used in the cartridges; and that didn't fit in with Omega's theory about inherited knowledge. Detroit had never been a munitions town, though it had experienced, and disastrously, the results of their manufacture. The gun itself held the answer to the puzzle. Bolt for bolt, and screw for screw, it was the exact duplicate of the actual guns which had been used in the last war.

If the thing had been something close to the original, he would have said that it represented a development of modern times. But this was *too* close for that. It was a copy, if it was not actually one of those in use over six thousand years ago, and preserved in some miraculous fashion to the present day.

Omega dropped the weapon and turned to the guards, just as the skinny man, who had not yet felt the power of Omega's mind, was drawing a careful bead on him with another gun.

"This is too much, really," Omega said and froze the man with his finger tight against the trigger. "Mustn't shoot people in the back. Didn't your mother ever teach you that?"

Gently, he probed the man's mind. Gently, because with the full force of his vast mental power, a weak human brain would be burned out in an instant. And this didn't look like a particularly bright specimen.

Surprisingly he learned that the man's mother *had* taught him not to shoot people in the back. She had, in fact, taught him to be a pretty good boy. Omega noted, still more puzzled, that the man wasn't essentially vicious. He really was an exemplary citizen. Nor could Omega, at first, find anything to account for his inhuman and unreasonable actions. Then he found it, stuck way down at the bottom of the man's subconscious, tucked away under a lot of old inhibitions and report cards. The man had a fixation, probably hypnotically induced.

But try as he might he could find no memory, conscious or subconscious, of the identity of the person who had imposed the fixation. There was merely the post-hypnotic command that the guard should open the gate to no one but those citizens who were able to give the proper passwords. Others were to be killed summarily. Arrows were to be used for the purpose unless they failed because of distance or armor.

Further, the rifles were never to be used in cases where their use might be observed by strangers too far away to be killed instantly.

CHAPTER II

METROPOLIS, 7952 A.D.

OMEGA SHOOK HIS head and turned to the other man. But he found the same thing there. Except that the skinny man was claustrophobic and had a mother complex. Neither man had any awareness of the hypnosis. Both would act normally up to the moment when someone unauthorized attempted to enter the gate. Then they would obey the hypnotic command.

Irritably and with a certain pettishness, Omega erased the influence of the former hypnosis, and replaced it with a command of his own: the guards were to open the gate freely to anyone who might approach. He chuckled to himself as he floated gently down from the top of the wall, into the city.

Omega noticed a change from his last visit. Then the city had been surrounded by miles of tilled and cultivated soil. Hundreds of soldiers were on constant guard duty throughout the area, protecting the fields from raids by savage nomads. But now the outposts of the city were on the walls themselves. The surrounding fields were no longer in use.

Just inside the walls of the city there lay a narrow strip, no more than a half-mile wide, which seemed to be intensely cultivated. A half-mile by about twenty miles—hardly enough to feed a city of such size. Omega noticed pipe-lines for irrigation. A constant mist seemed to be rising from these. He also noticed that at regular distances, on the city side of the narrow strip, were tall, windowless towers, surmounted by what appeared to be immense concave mirrors, pointing downward and outward over the cultivated area.

Omega decided that this needed looking into.

The nearest tower was a short distance away. He hobbled to its base and found a small, locked door. A push of a finger opened it. Its simple lock presented no difficulty to one whose vision was not limited to a medium with so many drawbacks as light, which refused to turn corners or penetrate through such porous materials as wood and iron.

When occasion demanded Omega could see, or hear, or feel, over such diversified media as cosmic rays, ultra violet, sonic waves and even gamma rays, all of which he could manufacture as needed.

The tumblers of the lock yielded instantly to his mental burglary and he mounted the pair of stairs which he found directly behind the door. He groaned as his creaky joints made audible protests. Omega delighted in an acting ability that was, if nothing else, unique. He lived his roles.

A HEAD poked forth from the top of the stairwell, and a pair of eyes widened in surprise. "I must have forgot to lock the door," muttered the head. Then aloud, "What do you want, old one?"

"A cup of coffee and a piece of apricot pie, please," said Omega amiably. A taste for apricots ranked high after curiosity in a list of Omega's vices.

"Never heard of either," said the man at the top. "You'd better get out of here. It's against the rules to allow anybody near the growth projector. Dangerous, too. There's leakage around that mirror, and it does something to your insides. We have to work in short shifts on account of it."

"I'm an old man anyway," remarked Omega, as he puffed up to the top and gazed at a roomful of machinery. "What's all this?"

"That's the machine that makes the growth ray," the man answered. "It's tuned to the potatoes. Turns out a new crop every two days. They dig them out at night, when the ray's shut off. Say, you must be a stranger in this city!"

"You couldn't tune it to apricot pies, I don't suppose. No. Pity. Great town you have here," Omega said, shifting his attention from the machinery, which he didn't understand, to the projection ray itself. He analyzed that briskly and identified it as a wave he had run across once before. It had been used by a highly advanced race living on one of the planets which encircled a sun a few hundred light-years distant. The ray was the result of a highly developed civilization, and he wondered at its presence here on a benighted earth.

"Down there," his guide went on, "are the pipelines which furnish the plants with water. Dissolved in the water are all the minerals needed to replace those that the plants take from the ground. Great invention. Vargo's work."

Omega noticed a slight spasm of pain cross the man's face as he talked. Curious, he probed with his versatile vision, into the man's body. He was disgusted to see a malignant, cancerous growth at work in the abdomen. Delicately he removed the growth, destroying it utterly, and healed the tissues which it had damaged.

"You'd better quit this job and get another," he advised, sounding like a personnel manager.

The man's face registered something akin to horror. "No, no!" he protested. "This is my life's work. I love it! It makes me mad that they won't let me stay here all the time. But two hours is the limit. And I guess they're right," he said, regretfully. "It seems that if a man stays here much longer, the leakage of the ray causes funny things to happen inside him."

Omega nodded. "There was an extremely funny thing inside of you, a minute ago. How long have you been doing this?"

"Four years."

There were some other things that Omega was curious about and he decided that questioning was too slow. The man stiffened when Omega looked deeply into his eyes. But Omega found practically the same thing that he had seen in the other two. This man was also under the influence of hypnosis. He firmly believed that he enjoyed the monotonous job of directing the growth ray. Yet there was no record in his brain of the identity of the one who had impressed this belief.

Omega did, however, discover one other fact. Each boy and girl of the city was given a fair education, and upon graduation was sent to a governmental unit which decided, ostensibly, what aptitudes were present and what line of work should be followed. Appropriately, this was called the Vocation Board. Training for the chosen profession followed. It was at this point, most likely, that the hypnotic suggestion had been planted.

In one way, Omega reflected, the practice was beneficial. It certainly made for satisfied and happy workers. But on the other hand it was tough on the lads who were given jobs like this one. Nor did it fall under the scope of Rugged Individualism, or the Democratic Principle.

OMEGA FROWNED, mentally of course, as the thought came that Mark wouldn't like it. And after all this was Mark's world, whether he wanted it or not. Omega had made him a present of it with fixtures and good will included, and it was up to Omega to see that it stayed the way Mark liked to have it. He decided to look a little further, before setting the machinery in motion which would bring this state of affairs to Mark's attention.

He restored the man's consciousness and bade him a cheerful goodbye. The growth ray operator didn't know it, but he now had another four years or so to enjoy his occupation. But then, he probably hadn't realized that his life expectancy had been numbered in days before Omega had run across him.

Omega penetrated deeper into the city, pausing from time to time, in an effort to satisfy his curiosity. The further he penetrated, the more puzzled he became.

There were a great many things which showed signs of being the result of unnatural progress. Others were normal developments of the millennium since he had observed the city. Multi-storied buildings could be expected, inasmuch as the city had not spread outward. Upward growth was normal, for a knowledge of engineering would develop during the same centuries which doubled and trebled the population.

In the matter of mechanical development, the city was in almost the same stage as it had been before the great war which destroyed it.

Omega became annoyed, as the day grew older, at his inability to ferret out the facts he sought. But so complete is the loss of memory incurred when a posthypnotic suggestion commands that the subject forget, that even Omega's great mind couldn't bring the forgotten facts to the fore. Knowledge of the hypnotist's identity had been erased so thoroughly that it might as well have never existed.

With his annoyance came a certain amount of alarm.

Several times he had noticed a trace of something sinister in the course of his mental probing. Most of these happy people, though quite carefree and friendly, had a fixation that it was their destiny to some day spread out and conquer the surrounding cities of the country—and eventually the entire world!

There was no malice in the thought. There was no picture in their minds of the horrible bloodshed and privation such a course would bring. There seemed to be only the altruistic desire to give the rest of the world the benefit of their own economic and social progress.

Omega, for the sake of his own curiosity, set out to find the headquarters of the Vocation Board. There, he knew, would be the answer to the whole puzzle.

As he searched, his mind dwelt upon another matter entirely. Mark, of course, would have to straighten things out in Detroit. On the other hand, there were certain matters a little closer to Mark's own home which needed straightening out also. Mark's two kids weren't getting any younger, and the race must be perpetuated... Maybe these two jobs could be dove-tailed.

CHAPTER III

THE CASE OF THE CHINESE WHALE

THE NORTH ATLANTIC, usually a pretty tempestuous stretch of water, was on its good behavior. Mark stood, legs braced, at the wheel of his ship and wondered why he should be having so much trouble on such a fine day.

There was a steady breeze from the stern and absolutely no reason why the boat shouldn't sail itself. But it wasn't doing that, not by a long sight. On the contrary, it was pitching and yawing as wildly as if it had encountered a typhoon.

Mark didn't know what to make of it. And it wasn't the only thing he had to bother him. Most important was trying to decide why he had ever left home at all. Things had been going along quite satisfactorily, and there was no valid reason why he should have left his happy home. He suddenly realized, spinning the wheel viciously to offset a nasty tendency his ship seemed to have acquired to head in the general direction of the north pole, that although he had invented several reasons why he should make a trip across the Atlantic Ocean, none of them amounted to a hill of beans.

That yarn he had told Nona, for instance.

"What do you want to go there for?" she had demanded. "There's nothing in America."

"You just don't know anything about it," he had told her. "The country as a whole, I mean. Sure, you know your home town and a bit of the surrounding territory, But America's a big place."

"But the Vikings," Nona had reminded him. "They're supposed to have seen a lot of it. They didn't think much of it."

"I've investigated that," he'd told her. "None of them ever got in more than a few miles, so that doesn't mean much. And they never really found anything even about the people they raided. They just grabbed and bashed worthy citizens in the head and ran. And those squareheads aren't competent observers."

"I thought you liked them."

"I do. But does that mean that I think they qualify as sociological experts!"

"How about your work?" she had asked, sharply.

That had almost stumped him. But he'd risen beautifully to the occasion. "I've gone far enough for the present. These people are still semi-barbarians, you know. And it wouldn't be safe to push them too fast. Social and economic progress should keep pace with mechanical advancement. I've already inaugurated too many twentieth-century ideas.

"The candlemakers guild has been on my neck ever since I built that generator with the waterpower turbine, and electrified the city. I tried to get them to change their vocation and take up the manufacture of electric lamps, but they tell me they can't make them out of whale blubber, of which they have a monopoly. Things like that are getting me down."

THE DISCUSSION had gone on like that for quite a while, until Nona had finally seen that, even with logic and reason to back her up, she was on the losing side. Mark was practically perfect—but he was after all, A Man. She'd stretched herself in front of a full-length mirror and then scowled ferociously.

"Never try to cramp their style, my mother always said," she observed tartly. "They'll come back, sooner or later, and when they do, he'll love you twice as much!"

"I hope your mother had better command of her pronouns," he snapped. Then he softened. "Don't get the notion that I want a vacation from you. I could manage that without crossing any oceans. Some of these Svenska girls are very cute, I've been told.

And don't make faces. I've got a real reason for this trip. Scandinavia, you know, is a very small portion of the world. And Omega intends that our descendants eventually take over the entire globe. So it is my plan to establish myself in a section of the western hemisphere. Dominate it, if necessary, and advance the civilization of that portion to a point where our immediate descendants can settle and multiply in comparative safety.

"It's my job to provide several progressive communities, just as we've done here with the Vikings. We can't disappoint Omega, you know."

"That old goon," Nona grumbled. Then she'd smiled, and they'd kissed, and after an appropriate interval, everything had been all right again.

Some of the things he'd told Nona, even though they were spur-of-the-moment inventions, were good ideas at that. For one thing he had been pushing the Norsemen too fast. Occasionally he had gummed up the machinery of local economics. Progress had to be made slowly.

The business of the healers had proven that. But fortunately he had seen it in time. He hadn't gone ahead and explained about germs and told them to forget all about evil spirits. The healers—venerable sages all—would have placed him in the booby-bin, even if they had to build one especially for the occasion.

But while he had had to handle them with kid gloves, he'd made considerable progress there, even so. He had proven that there was more than one kind of sickness, and that different types must be treated in different ways.

He'd showed them that the evil spirits which caused scurvy couldn't be handled in the same manner as the demons who took refuge in wounds and animal bites. Whereas one group of spirits had to be propitiated by feeding the victim certain greens the other must be dealt with firmly, even brutally at times. That sort of teaching had been well received and quite a few prospective corpses had recovered to go forth in their ships and make corpses of others.

Another good idea, Mark recalled as he fought with the wheel, had been the one about his project to provide another place for his descendants to live and thrive.

Twelve years ago, when Omega had awakened him from the nap which had taken him six thousand years and had supplied his blood with a radioactive element that rendered him immune from fatigue and all but invulnerable to ordinary injuries, he had told Mark that he'd only done so with the idea of starting a new race on the earth. He had taken Nona, a normal girl, and changed her physical chemistry so that she was capable of perpetuating the new race. He had chosen her because her innate characteristics were of the same high type as Mark's.

Their children would inherit none of the greed and lust for power which had caused most of the wars that invariably had stunted man's growth, for the simple reason that neither of them possessed any tendencies in that direction.

Physical and mental strength, coupled with an almost immortal longevity, would be their tools. But, and Mark knew that this was his job, a start must be made in several spots on the earth's surface at the same time.

FURTHER COGITATION was interrupted by the increasing necessity of keeping every sense alert to prevent his tiny craft from overturning completely. And now his tenancy of this particular part of the ocean was being disputed by a group of ferocious and apparently simple-minded whales. In spite of the fact that they could have picked any of several thousand square miles in which to swim, they perversely kept bobbing up right in the path of Mark's craft. Making faces at him.

Each and every one of them carried a gross tonnage which would have made a collision fatal. And final. With no concept of the laws of traffic or courtesy, they refused to stay put long enough for him to steer his way through them. They would make sudden dashes across his bow, apparently trying to see how close they could come without actually capsizing him. No doubt it was great sport for the whales, but Mark couldn't see any humor in it.

"Go away, you stupid fools. Get out of here," Mark bellowed.

Tremendous waves, caused by their passage, kept him fighting vainly for control of the boat. His craft bobbed like a cork in a hurricane. The beasts seemed to have no sense of propriety. No sense at all, in fact. They spun madly and kept returning for another try. There were still as many in front of him as there had been when he first sighted them.

"And you," he called to the one who seemed to be leading the cotillion, "stop making those insane faces. Don't leer at me—" He broke off, for he was almost sure that a whale never leers. Though, of course, he might be mistaken. His experience with whales was quite limited.

The feeling, however, persisted. Whales just did not behave like this. They were too darned big to be so playful. Dignity, he presumed, should be present in direct ratio to the volume. Pixies, for instance, had practically no dignity at all, while elephants were crawling with it. A whale, therefore....

The thought congealed considerably when one of the beasts, a very large one, placed itself directly in the path of the boat, and opened its mouth. Mark heaved mightily on the wheel and managed to steer past it. His whole craft could have passed within that mighty maw. Mark immediately revised his cynical ideas about Jonah.

He noticed that as he passed the monster, it snapped its mouth shut and looked decidedly chagrined. And Mark was absolutely certain that whales weren't capable of that emotion. An embarrassed whale. The idea was appalling. And silly. That whale was either polluted or—

Sighing unhappily, Mark relinquished his hold on the spokes of the wheel. He staggered to the rail and waited for developments. They weren't long in coming. With derisive flirts of their tails, the entire school of overgrown aquatic animals sounded, disappearing in unison.

With their going, the sea calmed abruptly and the boat settled down. Mark waited, halfway between resignation and anger and a kind of nervous dread. Resignation, because he hadn't really expected that things would be peaceful as long as they had; anger because of the silly trick that had been played on him, dread because he was sure that Omega was in the vicinity. Only Omega could have caused the peculiar activities he had just observed.

He looked out over the sea, expecting the disembodied intelligence to make his appearance in the guise of a crackpot sea monster of some sort, but nothing like that occurred.

HE WAS on the point of concluding that perhaps the whales had been genuine after all, when he heard a voice from the direction of the wheel.

"Ain't you-all gwine ter say hello?"

Mark wheeled. And saw, not a lovable old darky with a refreshing mint julep in either hand, but a distinctly sinister Oriental who probably could have scared the pants off Fu Manchu.

"H'y'all, honey chile?" inquired the mandarin.

Marked groaned. "That's terrible. That corny accent. No Southerner ever says you-all to just one person. I know because I went around with a girl from Alabama,"—he blinked—"six thousand years ago... What do you want?"

"I want to show you something. Detroit."

"I've seen it," Mark replied glumly. "Oho—it was you that made me think of this goofy trip, was it?"

"I had nothing to do with it, son. I just happened to observe something that ought to be corrected."

Mark nodded. "It's always that way," he said. "Well, what is it? What's the matter with Detroit?"

"Don't know exactly," confessed the Oriental. "But it's something that needs looking into. Detroit has suddenly become civilized!"

Mark raised an eyebrow, but held his peace.

"Yep. Truly civilized," continued Omega, "They've got to the point where they can't wait any longer. They've just got to give the world the benefit of their culture. Even if they have to shoot everybody who doesn't agree with them, in the process. And that's the final proof of a human civilization. The Romans did it, if you remember. So did the Persians and the Greeks.

"I wasn't there," denied Mark. "Besides, they were a bit primitive."

"They were human," Omega said. "And I *was* there. Identical species of animal, I assure you. And incidentally, you Americans had the same altruistic tendencies, you know. You weren't satisfied till you had civilized the Indians, though you had to feed half of them firewater and murder the other half."

"Let's talk about Detroit," said Mark. "Didn't I hear you say something about shooting? They've developed guns, eh?"

"Yeah, and a lot of other things. But I'd rather not tell you about it. You can see for yourself. This planet is your job, not mine. I'm just a spectator—I hope."

"You're an instigator," accused Mark. "But has it occurred to you that there are something like four thousand miles between here and Detroit? By the time I get there the war will be over."

"It hasn't started yet," Omega informed him. "And you're practically there now!"

Mark felt a sinking sensation in the pit of his stomach as the boat suddenly dropped out from beneath his feet! The mandarin and he, elbows locked, rose in the air to a height of several hundred feet and then sped forward at an alarming rate, directly away from the rising sun. Mark strove mightily to keep an expressionless face, but this experience was a little too trying for convincing calm. His eyes were streaming tears from the rush of air, but through the blur he could see the satisfied expression on the face of the Oriental.

The roaring, buffeting of the wind died abruptly. Mark understood that, even though he noted that their speed had apparently increased. The waves beneath were an endless, gray blur. Omega had merely included a portion of the surrounding air in the bubble of vibrant force which was carrying them along. It insulated them from the effects of their speed.

As they flew along Mark became aware of an acute and annoying humming sound. Under his breath the sinister mandarin was singing a few discordant bars of *Carry Me Back to Ole Virginny.*

"Michigan," Mark corrected hoarsely.

CHAPTER IV

CITY FOR MARS

"THIS," OMEGA FINALLY explained, "is the type of thing you should be able to do yourself, instead of playing around with a primitive sailboat. This form of levitation and locomotion is the simplest manifestation of *telekinesis*, an ability which is inherent in every mind, even the humble human one. Look at the old Babylonian wizards. What brains they had!"

"Do you mean that there were better brains then than there were during the twentieth century?" asked Mark incredulously.

"Well," Omega started, "I'm not sure what *you'd* call better. They were better in certain respects, and not so good in others.

"They were able to utilize, to a certain extent, all the latent powers of their minds. They could control all the wave-bands of the phenomenon known as *thought*. They were masters of *telepathy*. That's the second shortest of the thought waves. And they were masters of *hypnotism*, the longest of the thought waves. They could do a few things with *telekinesis*, also.

"Not much, I'll admit, considering the scope of that ability. They couldn't create matter from energy, or vice versa, but that was mainly because humans don't live long enough to fully develop their powers. But some of these wizards did learn how to transport themselves from place to place, which is more than you have done.

"Even so I'd hesitate to say that their minds were superior. You see, the civilization of the twentieth century concentrated on developing one portion of the mind, and they didn't do so badly—for humans.

"Your people far outstripped the Babylonians in reasoning power. You explored realms in which the Babylonian merely scratched the surface. Mathematics, astronomy, physics, and such. That is why your people built a mechanical civilization.

"But you were only tapping one band of the thought group, that of reason and logic. The complete intelligence should be adept in the use of *all* of the brain's powers. If you had learned to really control the *telekinesis* band, you wouldn't need your mechanisms, not even the simple boat. And you'd be able to create the most complicated structure, using only the boundless energy of space as your building blocks and tools."

For some minutes they rushed along in silence. In the distance Mark could see the shore line of America's Atlantic coast. He was about to speak when Omega interrupted the attempt.

"I hope that's sinking in," he said. "Twelve years ago I tickled that portion of your brain which emits the waves of *hypnosis*. How many times have you used the ability?"

"Four or five times," answered Mark. "But then there's been no need. I wouldn't use it on anybody except in an emergency. Wouldn't be fair."

"There you go, you ingrate! If you don't use it, you can't develop it. Not fair, eh? Well, for cat's sake. Was it fair for a brainy man to use his powers to acquire a fortune, when his less intellectual brothers starved?"

"That's different," Mark claimed. "That's ordinary competition."

"Ordinary competition, eh? If you ask me, it's just that one man used his equipment and the other was too lazy. But the point is that you have failed to exercise the ability I gave you. Yet I'll bet you're on the point of asking me to tickle the *telekinesis* portion of your brain, so that you can get about quicker. Well, I won't do it!"

MARK WATCHED Mount Desert slide past beneath him.

"Well I *was* going to ask you," he admitted. "But then this is not a thing which I'd have to use in competition with anyone. That's why I've seldom used hypnotism. In a fair fight each fighter has to have the same weapons. And that's a weapon the other fellow never seems to possess."

"You should be wearing your old school tie, you Rover Boy." Omega chuckled. "Wait'll you get to Detroit," he said, enigmatically. "But you're all off again. *You* haven't fought a fair fight in years. *You've* always had an advantage.

"The other guy didn't have the kind of blood which would heal a wound instantly, did he? He didn't have muscles which were eternally rejuvenated by a radioactive element in his blood, did he?

"No, he got tired, like any weak human. He was licked before he started. You've got to get it into your head that all competition resolves itself into a battle between two *unequal* forces. The better equipped force wins, barring unforeseen accidents. And the weaker force invariably thinks it is the stronger, or it wouldn't seek a battle.

"So when you get embroiled in any sort of competition, always use every weapon you have. To do less only prolongs the agony of the other guy."

Mark listened, and in the main agreed, though with certain mental reservations. Though he had to privately admit that he had never fought anybody who didn't think he was a pushover. The apparent odds had always been on the other fellow's side. Which had conveniently removed Mark's scruples about taking advantage of his superior equipment.

"You know," said Mark. "This ability to move about at high speeds without an airplane would come in handy if I'm to keep an eye on developments here on the earth. Things like this Detroit business wouldn't be so apt to escape me."

"None of your Blarney," Omega snorted. "I won't lift a finger. You've got to develop it for yourself."

"But I don't know how to get started," Mark complained. "It's like trying to play a piano with your toes. Only a few people can do it, and yet all people have the proper muscles. The trouble is that they don't know how to use them. The nerves are atrophied, or something. Same thing with this *telekinesis*. You say my brain is capable of manipulating the energies of space. That may be so, fast enough, but I don't know how to do it. And I can't learn unless I get a start... I'll tell you—I'll make a bargain with you."

The Oriental features took on an interested expression. "I'se a listenin', white boy," said Omega.

"Will you cut that out? Well, when you gave me the use of that portion of my brain which emits hypnosis waves, you developed the faculty to perfection. All in one dose. I didn't have to do a thing. Now with this *telekinesis* faculty, suppose you just excite that region of my brain sufficiently for me to realize the sort of effort needed to exercise it. Then I'll do the rest myself. I'll develop it from scratch, without any more help."

Omega didn't answer immediately. "It doesn't seem quite like a bargain," he mused. "What do I get?"

"You gave me a job to do here, didn't you?" Mark pressed. "It was all your idea to provide Nona with the same kind of blood as mine, so that the earth would eventually become populated with a more durable species of human. And you've appointed me to see that things don't happen the way they always have when humans became wise enough to annihilate each other. So you should help provide me with the tools to carry out the project. You can't beat logic, you know."

"No, but you *can* twist it all out of shape," said Omega. "That's a habit of yours... I don't know why I ever monkeyed in human affairs anyway. Once you start, you can't stop. All right, chuckle-head, I'll operate on you."

LAKE ONTARIO and Lake Erie had slid beneath as they talked, and Mark noticed that they were now poised almost directly above the Detroit River, once called the Dardanelles of the New World. On its western shore sprawled the new Detroit, and at the sight of it Mark forgot all about Omega's promise. For Mark had once, six thousand years before, flown in a transport plane over that city, and it had looked almost the same as it did now!

A sudden wave of nostalgia gripped him at the sight of factories belching smoke, and automobiles speeding along the broad streets. Since his awakening, twelve years before, he had only experienced this feeling a few times, and then he had been too busy to let it bother him. But then it was only his memory that had made him homesick.

Here was something much stronger. Here was an American city in full throb of prosperous industry. A piece of the twentieth century transplanted into the eightieth!

It was almost too much.

Omega must have sensed something amiss, for he took immediate action to cure the disease.

Mark felt a sudden rush of air, accompanied by the same all-gone feeling in the pit of his stomach which had accompanied his rise from the deck of the ship. But this time he was descending, and much faster than he had gone up. His course was a slanting one, aimed in the general direction of a building on one of the busier streets. Alarmed, he noticed that he no longer felt the restraining arm of Omega. Frantically he looked around.

Omega was gone!

HE EXPERIENCED an instant of panic as the building became larger and closer. Then he smiled, albeit a bit sickishly. Falling bodies went straight down—apparently, at least. He wasn't doing that, and therefore wasn't a falling body. His descent was being directed. Which meant that his friend had merely abandoned his human form and was in his natural disembodied state.

Mark was right. His slanting course carried him down into the canyon of the street barely clearing the roof of a skyscraper. "Whoops!" he yelped nervously. His descent became as vertical as the fall of a stone. Then, a few feet from the pavement he stopped plummeting and went swooping through the doorway of a store on the street level.

He caught a fleeting vision of a sign which read *Apparel for Misses* and his heart sank. He knew what was coming as well as if he had seen a moving picture of it. For Omega had little respect for the conventions of humans. Anatomy was anatomy to him and gender merely an affectation.

This was bad!

Mark's blurring flight didn't stop in the store immediately until he had soared the whole length of the store and crashed through a French door at its end. He landed with grace and precision directly in the center of three ladies of almost certain age who were trying on various intimate items of women's apparel. Three screams in different keys rent the air as Mark wheeled like a dervish and made for the shattered door. He passed through it even faster than he had come in, pursued by outraged female yelps.

Mark slowed to a walk as he reached the street. Curious stares greeted him in the vicinity of the store-front, but as he walked down the street they died away and Mark breathed a sigh of relief.

"You applebrain!" came a harsh whisper in his ear. "I operated on you just before I dropped you. I gave you the power you asked for, and did you make the slightest use of it? Not you! The way you've started you'll never make even a halfway decent Mercury to my Jupiter. See if you can improve by the time I get back. And look out for Vargo! Whoever he is. Toodle-ooo."

THE VOICE trailed off in the sounds of traffic. Mark looked around him observing the people who thronged the sidewalks. He was pleased to note that, contrary to twentieth-century practice, the men were far more scantily clothed than the women. Since he wore nothing above the waist and only short leather breeches below, it was just as well that the male Detroiters were not turned out much more completely.

Because of the radioactivity of his blood, Mark wore the same garments, winter and summer. Trunks and a pair of sandals provided all the covering he needed or wanted. A broad belt, which bolstered his axe and dagger, completed the costume.

It was warmish and most of the men he saw wore trunks, like his own. Some had belts, slightly narrower than his, which contained short-swords and automatic pistols. Soldiers or police, he decided. The others were unarmed.

Mark attracted little attention; but there were a few curious, even suspicious, looks directed at his axe. Axes evidently weren't standard weapons in these parts. More curiosity was evinced when people happened to notice his dented, but shiny, winged helmet. That, very likely, had no counterpart in the city of Detroit. But Mark was determined not to part with it, even if it did make him conspicuous. That helmet had protected his skull though through many a battle and he had a certain understandable attachment for it.

He was considering the possibility of passing himself off as one of the constabulary in order to pick up few vital statistics, when the thing was settled for him. A young man equipped with short-sword, pistol and a smooth helmet which resembled the coal-scuttle variety used by the Germans in the first World War, stopped before him and respectfully saluted.

"I'm a recruit in the First Division, sir," he said, eyeing Mark's accoutrements uncertainly. "Can you tell me… You *are* an officer, aren't you?"

Mark smiled indulgently, his mind racing at top speed as he hesitated before answering. The man's clipped shorthand English was intelligible though it was quite changed from the twentieth-century language he had known. Mark knew that he could duplicate it without any trouble. He'd had a lot of practice in learning new dialects in the past twelve years. But the trouble was that he had no notion of what to say. He decided to take a chance.

"A commander, sonny," he answered. "Mercury Division. What's on your mind?"

THE MAN responded with a friendly, though slightly puzzled smile. "I haven't heard of that one, sir," he said. "Everything seems to be so upside down these days that nobody knows exactly what's going on. I guess that'll all be straightened out, though. But what I need to know is when I'm to report again. They shooed us out so quick when they issue our swords and guns, that nobody remembered to tell us. I tried to get back in, but when the guard saw my equipment he just waved me away. There was such a crowd at the recruiting station that I had to give it up. Do you know when we start our march?"

Mark nodded. "You'll be notified when to appear for further orders," he said. "You'll have to be trained a little, you know."

The man's eyes widened. "Trained? I never heard of that. I thought that we were to march in a week or so."

"Did you say you were just recruited today?" asked Mark.

The man nodded. "I understand the recruits are to be placed under the leadership of seasoned men from the caravan guards. They know how to handle the nomads and they will be our officers when we attack other cities."

Mark bit back his astonishment. Raw recruits sent to war, without training, with caravan guards as officers! An armed mob nothing more.

Then Mark remembered the primitive state of the nomadic tribes which roamed the countryside, and decided that maybe an armed mob would do the trick nicely. On the other hand the nomads were fighters and a good many of these recruits were sure to be slaughtered, even though they were armed with guns.

"You'll be notified," he repeated. "Keep close to home."

"I hope it's soon," asserted the youth, an ecstatic expression on his face. "Our civilization will lift the world from savagery! This generation will go down in history. Vargo's name will be glorified forever. The Ancestors will be proud!"

CHAPTER V

THE ANCESTORS LIVE

MARK WALKED ALONG and tried to make some sense out of what he had heard. The projected campaign was imminent, that seemed certain. Yet the whole affair seemed to be being slapped together in the most half-baked sort of way.

Could it be that the powers who were running the show, this Vargo for instance, had no conception of the necessary approach to a war of conquest? It certainly looked like it. Young men who probably had never handled a weapon in their lives were blithely babbling about conquering the world. Of course they might be able to pull it off, considering the guns and automobiles; but most of them would wish they had never heard of a war, before they were through.

Then there was that mention of the Ancestors.

The youth had pronounced the word with a decided degree of reverence. It had sounded to Mark like a form of religion, though ancestor-worship and progress never had gone hand-in-hand, as far as he knew. There was nothing to do but try to gather further information and improvise from there.

Mark, idly walking down the street and pondering his next move, fell to inspecting the types of cars and trucks which passed up and down the city's busy streets.

By the sound of the motors, they were almost all high-powered vehicles, yet there seemed to have been little attempt made on the part of the designers to make them look well. This may have been partly due to the fact that most of them were trucks and strictly utilitarian; but their design would make a Model T look like a gleaming Rolls by comparison. Even the passenger cars. They were all squarish, and built on the general lines of taffy boxes. Closer inspection made him think that this might be because of old-fashioned methods used in the stamping mills. The bodies weren't stamped in one piece, but rather were welded together from a dozen or more pieces.

Mark paused at the next corner and waited for a break in the stream of vehicles. Several others were waiting, more patiently than he. There seemed to be no traffic system worthy of the name. True, there was a policeman on the corner, but he seemed to be doing nothing in the way of giving the pedestrian even a good opening. He merely observed the movements of the vehicles and occasionally waved his hand to hurry the speed of a car or truck coming from the lesser-used side street.

But he made no attempt to halt traffic on the larger of the two streets. Cars on the smaller one sped across as the opportunity offered. As near as Mark could tell this larger street had a definite right of way over the smaller. And pedestrians had no rights at all. It wasn't so different from the twentieth century, and at least you knew definitely where you stood.

The policeman refused to do a thing to give them an opportunity to cross. Yet surprisingly, they didn't seem to resent, this in the least. They appeared perfectly content to await their chance to make a dash for it.

MARK WAS suddenly distracted by a loud yell from the policeman. It was accompanied by lesser yells from several of the pedestrians. An old man, who had been waiting on the opposite side of the larger street, thought he saw an opportunity to scurry across. Several others took the same chance. But in the center of the street one of the younger men in the group jostled against the old one and tripped him.

The oldster fell heavily, directly in the path of a huge truck!

Squealing brakes mingled with the shouts of pedestrians. Mark didn't yell. He acted.

With a speed born of tireless, steel-spring muscles, he leaped in front of the truck and snatched the old man to safety. He carried him to the pavement and stood him upright. He tried to inquire if the oldster had been hurt, but his voice made not a dent in the din raised by dozens of horns and a score or so of angry voices.

The horns subsided as the trucks hurried on. But the voices became louder. Mark, for a minute, couldn't make it out. The people, instead of being glad that the old man had escaped death, were angry that he had delayed traffic for an instant! The oldster cringed at their insulting tirades. Mark patted him reassuringly on the shoulder and turned to face the irate policeman who was approaching.

"Doddering old fool!" raged the cop. "If you're too feeble to cross a street, why don't you use the underpass?"

"Where's the underpass?" asked Mark, somewhat out of patience, himself.

"A half mile up the street," quavered the old man. "A hundred steps down and then a hundred steps up again. My legs aren't up to it."

"Makes no difference," rasped the officer. "You'll face the tribunal for delaying traffic!"

A murmur of approval came from the crowd of onlookers as the cop reached forth a hand to take the old one's arm. Mark struck it away.

"Not so fast," he said. "The man was knocked down. He couldn't help delaying your precious traffic."

The cop flushed from his eyebrows to his short ribs, which were exposed.

"Wise guy, huh? Okay, for that I'll take you along, too. Assaulting an officer!"

The officer evidently thought his pistol would be needed for the job, for he began to draw it. That was a mistake.

In an instant he was flat on his back and Mark was dusting off his knuckles and grinning at the glazed look in the cop's eyes.

The latter made an effortful and badly coördinated attempt to pull himself together, gave it up as a bad job, and subsided peacefully on the pavement.

Mark's grin faded at the sound of the gasp of horror which arose from the onlookers. He turned to face them, wondering what manner of people inhabited this modern city of Detroit. They certainly weren't behaving as normal urbanites. In his day a cheer would have greeted the manhandling of a cop who had acted like this one.

He noticed that the crowd was composed mainly of young people, with apparently only a few over fifty. These few, he was pleased to see, were smiling happily. The rest were frowning and muttering threateningly.

"You inhuman brats," Mark told the latter. "This old man might have been the father of any of you. Out of the way, now, or I'll lay some of you out beside the cop."

THE CROWD parted reluctantly and he piloted the old man down the street. At the next corner he turned, looking back for an instant to see if there was any pursuit. There wasn't. Evidently the cop hadn't recovered and none of the others cared to invite similar treatment. He slowed his fast pace to allow the old man to catch his breath.

"Where are you headed for, Pop?" he asked. "I'll stay with you and see that you get there."

"Another block," said the oldster. "You took a terrible chance, young man. I'm very grateful. But more than that, I'm pleased. I thought that Vargo had stamped out such things as respect for one's elders. You must be a stranger in this city. What is your name? Mine is Dodd."

"Mark. And you're right. I am a stranger. But what's all this about a lack of respect for elders? I should expect the opposite. I heard some talk of ancestor worship in this city."

The old man shuddered. "The Ancestors!" he whispered, with something like loathing in his voice. "They're a blight on humanity! They fostered all this. They dream of a perfect world, yet they couldn't make a perfect one in their own time. Their progress is all a sham, a thing of no substance. It is bringing only misery, because it leads to the one thing that made theirs an imperfect civilization. War!

As he said the last, the old man turned into the doorway of a two-story structure. A small sign, etched in brass, proclaimed that the place was a home for the aged.

Dodd led the way into a large room which looked like a combination library and recreation room. For an instant Mark fancied himself transported six thousand years into the past and set down inside a YMCA.

One wall was lined with bookcases, and scattered here and there were tables where men played chess, checkers and cards. The men were all aged, yet appeared like any similar group of his own time. There were kindly-looking men with silky white beards, crabbed-appearing ones, and tired, spiritless ones.

Here and there were notes of incongruity. The cards weren't the same as those of the twentieth-century sort, and the chess boards had twice as many pieces, And there were a few games that he failed to recognize at all.

Books, on the other hand, were the same. Probably the present-day civilization had developed along lines similar to his own because of the many things which had been salvaged from the ruins after the end of the last wars. The art of bookmaking may have been one of the salvaged processes. Though, of course, the thing might be an accidental development, the result of progress in similar peoples reaching approximately the same point.

"The men you see here," Dodd said, "number more than half of the completely sane and free mentalities in this entire city!"

MARK GAZED about him, quite astonished. There weren't any more than fifty men in the large room. Some of them were looking at him in polite curiosity. Physically a young man, he did look out of place here in a roomful of the aged and feeble.

"Perhaps I'd better explain," said Dodd, indicating a chair.

"These men were in their forties when Vargo instituted his

new idea of vocational training. And that is why they are among the few remaining entirely sane people in this city. Vargo...."

"Wait a minute," interrupted Mark. "Let's start at the beginning. Who the devil is Vargo? I've been hearing a lot about that character."

Dodd made a wry expression. "Vargo, Giver of Life!" he said, sarcastically. "He's well on the way to becoming a god, right now. But those who knew him before he gained power consider him a grasping, egotistical tyrant. Something which should be eliminated for the betterment of the city.

"We, however, are in the minority. We number about a hundred as opposed to two million or so who think him almost divine.

"Our government used to be something on the order of those ancient republics you have probably read about. Our citizenry elected its king once every ten years. It did, that is, until Vargo came along. A business depression preceded his election, and his scientific methods ended it. He made drastic changes in social organization and in a very short time everybody was prosperous and happy. Happier than ever before. Result; no more elections. Vargo is king as long as he lives."

Mark's eyebrows lifted as he waited for some more. But Dodd, with senile absentmindedness, seemed to have sunk into a gloomy reverie.

"Pardon me," ventured Mark, and waited until Dodd's eyes raised to regard him glassily. "Vargo—remember?"

"Yes... Vargo! The scheming, sadistic. But you don't understand. We are not really prosperous. Our people are merely contented with much less than before. That is why they are happy. They don't have much, but they don't want much. Vargo has increased working hours and the people like it because everyone now enjoys his work! All they want is the opportunity to work longer hours, and they're deliriously happy about it!"

Mark shook his head and wondered if the old fellow had told

the truth about the state of sanity of those who met in this room. Somebody certainly was crazy.

"Sounds like an unusual state of affairs," he remarked.

Dodd nodded gloomily. "It's not natural," he said, resentfully.

"You men don't happen to be oldtime union organizers, do you?" Mark inquired.

Dodd seemed to be mystified at this. Mark concluded that the present civilization hadn't got quite that far. And if everyone liked his work as much as Dodd claimed, unions would never develop.

"Just what is your main objection to this Vargo?" he asked.

Dodd looked at him in amazement. "Why, because he is responsible for all this. He brought the Ancestors to life. He caused our people to think of nothing but production, production, production… That's why I was almost arrested. I was delaying production.

"If I slowed a couple of trucks for a few seconds, the materials which those trucks carried would be a few seconds late in arriving. And the factories to which they were going would be a few seconds later in using those materials to manufacture guns and other war equipment. It's getting so that human life is nothing compared to high-geared production. And the people want it that way!

Mark frowned. "Something's getting past me," he said. "Let's go back. What have the Ancestors to do with this? What did you mean by saying that Vargo brought them to life?"

A COMMOTION at the door prevented Dodd from answering. An elderly attendant raised his voice in quavering protest as several men pushed their way past him. Mark saw that they were police, or perhaps soldiers. Then he recognized the cop who had stopped his right hook. "That's him!" cried the policeman, pointing to Mark. "I remember that axe. And there's the old man, too."

Mark jumped to his feet as the police surged forward. He grinned as he noticed that there were only five of them. Fair enough odds, he thought. Should make a nice little pile on the floor.

But his grin faded when he saw them draw their pistols. He considered briefly the chances of dodging between bullets fired from five guns at once. Then he happened to think of the usual fate of innocent bystanders. That was really what made him raise his hands in surrender. He didn't relish the thought of any of the old men stopping a bullet intended for him.

Dodd was quivering with excitement as they were led toward a closed truck at the curb. Mark was slightly annoyed because he had permitted the officers to remove his weapons. But he consoled himself with the thought that he didn't really need them anyway.

"This is the last ride," Dodd quavered, as one of the police pushed him inside. "Vargo himself handles all cases involving malcontents. A thief would fare better."

Mark eased himself off a splinter in the rough bench, which ran the length of the truck's interior. This conveyance, he was thinking, was a poor imitation of the jiffy wagons of the twentieth century.

For although they hadn't been exactly luxurious, they had at least been equipped with padding on the seats. And the springs had been better. But then, some of the best people had ridden in them. Maybe it was different now.

"Keep your chin up, Pop," he advised. "I was going to drop in on Vargo, anyway. By the way, we were interrupted. What were you going to say? About Vargo, you know, bringing the Ancestors to life...."

DODD SHOOK his head wonderingly. "You're a strange man," he said. "Vargo is a scientist. He worked with electricity back in the days when little was known about it. I remember when he and I were in the same class in physics... But you wouldn't be interested in that....

"At any rate, Vargo discovered some kind of vibration which would reassemble the atoms of a decomposed body and bring it back to its original form. He did that when he was still in college. He had failures without number, producing freaks of all sorts. Foreign elements would be acted upon by his vibration and reconstruct all sorts of things within the bodies of the animals he experimented upon.

"For years none of them lived. He was finally successful when he turned his ray upon the contents of a bronze casket which had been dug up from one of the ancient cemeteries.

"A man was reconstructed, and he lived! Though he died shortly after from the effects of some copper oxide which had been restored within his body. The oxide from the casket had mingled with the remains of the body.

"And so, though he didn't give up, he met failure again.

"But Vargo was entirely successful when he tried his vibration on the contents of a casket made of one of the rustless steel compounds. That man became the first Ancestor. He restored others, five altogether, each one a specialist in some particular branch of science in which the ancients excelled. He put them to work, and they have done much to advance science and industry.

"Motor trucks have replaced horse-drawn vehicles within the city. Guns have come into existence. And about ten years ago one of the Ancestors invented the ray for forcing vegetable growth. Old-fashioned farming was abandoned, and we now grow enough to feed the city, entirely within the walls. Even the enormous quantities of vegetable matter that is fermented to produce the alcohol for the motors.

"Vargo took the credit for most of the work of the Ancestors, which they don't seem to mind, and as a result he was elected king. And he became so popular that no more elections have been held. For thirty years, during which time the face of the city has changed tremendously, he has used the science of the Ancestors to further his own ambitions."

The old man fell into a fretful silence, watching the progress of the patrol wagon through a barred window. Mark was equally silent, for there was a lot to think about.

CHAPTER VI

WITHOUT WINGS, YOU FLY

IT WAS ALMOST too much to digest at one sitting. Especially considering the available accommodations for sitting. It was enough to give one an ache in various places.

Dead men brought back to life! Dead for quite some time, too. Living ancestors! And they actually were that, for the bodies had been dug up from the very graveyards which the remote ancestors of these people had used.

The mention of stainless steel caskets gave Mark to believe that the Ancestors must be from a period only slightly later than his own former existence. Rustless metals had come into wide usage during the years preceding the beginning of his long sleep. Therefore these Ancestors had lived, sometime during that century, at the height of Man's conquest of Science. No wonder Vargo had put them to profitable use.

That raised another question. Why did they allow him to do so? Did Vargo's plans match their own aims? Or did he have some hold over them?

Mark was about to ask when the patrol wagon bumped over a curbing and heaved itself up a driveway. Dodd and he were kept covered by the policemen's pistols as they got out. Then they were herded through a door and down a corridor lined with cells. Mark frowned at the sight of them.

"Take us to Vargo," he demanded.

The answer to that was a sudden rush by three policemen, at the conclusion of which Mark found himself on the less pleasing side of a cell door. It clanged decisively shut. Decisively, that is, from the viewpoint of the police. Cell doors are supposed to be that way. This one, for some reason wasn't. They were more than surprised to see it bounce open as quickly as it had closed! The foremost cop slammed it shut again, even harder than before. That was a tactical error, for it only bounded back harder. It caught him before he could get out of the way and knocked him flat.

Mark stepped back, deeper into the darkness of his cell, and thus farther from the door. He didn't want to be in the way should it suddenly decide to swing inward. From his personal experience with cell doors he knew that they were unpredictable. Omega, you see, liked to play with them when he was around.

Mark remembered one which had turned a cherry red, and then melted at his feet.

This one, however, did no such a thing. It completed its swing, banged against the wall and then returned slowly and locked itself. The policemen, looking puzzled and pretty sullen, retired from the immediate vicinity, first cautiously closing the door of another cell on the unfortunate Dodd.

Mark listened to their footsteps march down the corridor and cease with the closing of a door at its end. "Come on, you old fox," he coaxed. "Make yourself visible."

"Haven't time," said a soft voice close to his ear. "I just dropped in to see how you're doing. And as usual, I find you in jail. What are you, anti-social?"

"They got a law here against socking cops," Mark explained.

"Narrow-minded, eh? What have you done about telekinesis?"

MARK GROANED. "I was afraid you'd bring that up. Here it's been two hours since you allegedly operated on me, and I haven't done a thing. I can't even melt those cell doors. I guess I'm a failure."

"Two hours is a long time," Omega stated. "I went clear to

Andromeda, several hundred light-years away, and back in that interval."

Mark affected a yawn. "Interesting," he commented. "And how are all the folks on dear old Andromeda? It's been quite some time since I've...."

"Cut it out, nitwit," Omega snapped. "I told you I'm short of time. But I just happened to remember that I didn't finish that operation."

"That's why I said 'alleged,'" Mark said. "I didn't feel anything."

"You wouldn't," said Omega. "I operated on that portion of your brain which controls the energies locked in the sub-etheric vibrations. You now have enough development to use them to move matter. That's all, though. I didn't develop it enough to allow you to create or destroy matter. You'll be able to do that yourself, if you practice for a few hundred years. But I forgot something. Remember the time I developed your hypnotic ability?"

Mark nodded, knowing that Omega could see him even though he couldn't see Omega.

"At that time," Omega went on, "I found it necessary to throw my own hypnosis wave against you in order to start you resisting me. That gave you the stimulus which enabled you to get the feel of handling your own wave. Now the point is, having developed your telekinesis center how shall we stimulate it?"

Mark was stumped.

Years ago, before his blood had become the self-rejuvenating fluid he now possessed it had been necessary for him to sleep. And he remembered that he used to dream. One of his most frequent dreams had been of flying. Sometimes he had done this by flapping his arms, as if they were wings. But more often he had just held his arms at his sides and wished—wished most mightily—that he were moving through the air. And he had moved.

He told Omega about it.

"That's no good," claimed Omega. "A race memory, nothing

more. You humans were once flying reptiles, and you still wish you had wings."

OMEGA WAS silent for a few minutes after that. And being invisible, he seemed to have left entirely. Mark was on the point of calling to him when he felt himself rise a few inches from the floor. His arms churned for a moment as he felt himself tipping sideways. It didn't do any good; he still tipped. He buckled his knees, trying to reach the floor with his feet, but they stayed up.

He was about to relax and lean against the force which was keeping him in a slanting position, when abruptly it tipped him over in another position.

"No, you don't!" came the voice in his ear. "Come on, use your brain. You're standing on a tilting floor and I won't let you off it until you manage to rise of your own accord. I won't let you fall, but I won't let you stand straight either."

The tilting position was doing something to Mark's sense of balance. Omega wouldn't keep him tilted in one direction long enough for him to get accustomed to it, and his stomach didn't like it a bit. Only the fact that he hadn't eaten anything for over twelve years kept it from turning over entirely. But that didn't prevent him from feeling quite dizzy and nauseated. He fought the sensation and tried to do something about it.

The effort was futile until he happened to think of his dreams. Then he tried placing his hands at his sides and wishing he could fly. That didn't work either. He stayed on the invisible, tipped platform.

Experimentally he closed his eyes and tried to capture the feeling he had experienced in his dreams. Wishing alone wouldn't do the trick, he realized. He remembered back to the days when he had dreamed those dreams. It had been during his life in the twentieth century. He hadn't slept once since that six-thousand-year nap.

Hazily, eyes still closed, he pictured those dreams: Always he had sensed a certain liquid quality in the surrounding atmosphere. Then he remembered clearly had that property of fluidity been a latent realization of the presence of those sub-cosmic vibrations which abound in all space. Was it some race memory of a time when his ancestors had been able to utilize those waves? He didn't know, but tried mightily to recapture the sensation.

Possibly it was because his eyes were closed; possibly because Omega knew of his struggle and was helping, but in a few minutes he became aware of the liquid quality he sought.

Immediately he imagined himself rising, and then suddenly his eyes were jarred open by a resounding thump on his head. He had hit the ceiling! That little incident unnerved him to the extent that he lost all thought of his control of the levitation principle, and he crashed to the floor in a loose heap of arms and legs and angry curses.

The chuckle that came from the air near his left ear was hearty and appreciative. "Nice doing, son," Omega congratulated. "But you have to keep your mind on your work. Try it again, this time with your eyes open. You can feel the waves which surround you now. It'll be easy."

Mark scrambled to his feet, somewhat groggily. Omega was right. He could feel the waves.

Even with his eyes open and fully awake, he sensed that he was immersed in an all-pervading bath of cosmic emanations. That was the secret of the thing; the consciousness of those waves. Once you could feel them you could use them. Before he had been like a blind man, knowing that there was light but unable to see it.

Omega had made him able to see.

CAUTIOUSLY HE willed to rise from the floor. Slowly but steadily the ceiling came nearer. Then he thought of stopping his ascent and moving horizontally. His body obeyed his will and approached the far wall. He stopped abruptly and descended to the floor, looking wildly around for Omega before he remembered that he was still disembodied.

"But I have no consciousness of directing these waves!" he said, excitedly. "I just thought of rising and the waves lifted me!"

"Sure, sure," said the voice, patiently. "When you want to wiggle your fingers, your brain doesn't consciously direct each action of all the muscles involved. You just think of it and they wiggle. A baby has to learn, of course, but after a few tries the muscles obey from force of habit. Trial and error in the beginning; later, habit.

"There is never any stage where the brain is completely conscious of all the movements of the muscles. When you move your wrist, for instance, a muscle in your forearm does the work, yet your brain isn't aware of it. When, you take a breath you are really expanding your ribs by an action of the muscles between them. You don't suck the air in; the enlarged chest cavity creates a partial vacuum and the air rushes in because the pressure is greater outside.

"It's the same with *telekinesis*. With your consciousness of the waves comes the automatic ability to manipulate them. Later, of course, you may learn to sense some of the peculiar properties of those waves and make them do some of the things I can make them do. That, however, will take a lot of practice and you'll have to do it yourself. I refuse to help you any more!"

While Omega talked Mark exultantly wafted himself about through the air in his cell. He moved erratically, first with extreme caution, then with increasing confidence. In a minute or two he was darting from wall to wall and making abrupt turns at high speed. A bat could have done no better.

"What did my dreams have to do with it?" he finally asked.

"That's got me stumped," Omega confessed. "Fifty thousand years ago I left my body and started to roam around the universe. At that time the continent of Atlantis was going through the throes which resulted in its submergence to the bottom of the Atlantic. I never did get a chance to observe its peoples. Some of them escaped by reason of the fact that they were traveling in far lands at the time. They became your ancestors, no doubt.

"Maybe they had the power of telekinesis, later losing it from intermarriage with more primitive peoples and descending once again to savagery. That would account for your race memory of soaring. It's hard to say, though. Human history is so confusing. Nothing like my own people, who developed constantly as the Moon aged, from primitive organisms to highly intelligent beings. You humans have gone up and then down again so many times that it's hard to tell what may have happened."

Mark described a few more revolutions about the room, too busy to make a remark. But he quickly remembered Omega when he felt himself pressed downward until he was prone on the floor, pressing against the rough cement.

"Upstart!" grated the voice in his ear. "Don't get too cocky about all this. I'm still Jupiter around here."

"Okay, Jupe," gasped Mark. "You don't have to prove it. Ease up."

The pressure vanished and Mark bounded to his feet.

He waited for a minute and when no comment was forthcoming, he cautiously called Omega's name. No answer; Omega had gone about his mysterious business. Mark shook his head in bafflement. Omega liked to linger and talk but sometimes he seemed to be in a burning rush. And this was evidently one of those times. Though why Omega should be in a hurry, with all eternity before him, Mark couldn't imagine....

CHAPTER VII

HE FLOATS THROUGH THE AIR

MARK IDLY INSPECTED the bars of his cell. He tried to make some sense out of the various things he had learned in the short time since he had dropped in on the city of Detroit. The people, it seemed, were wholly entranced with Vargo. They not only failed to resent the fact that he had increased their working hours, but they seemed heartily to concur in the idea.

Mark scowled. Man has never been a being to like work for the sake of work. A man will labor like a beaver to better himself, but according to Dodd, these people were so absorbed in their labor that they took interest in little else. And that was certainly peculiar. It all gave Mark a definite impression that all was not jake in the metropolis of Detroit.

As long as the people were happy, though, Mark saw no particular reason to interfere. But how long would they stay that way?

Dodd had said that all this rush of industry was for the purpose of preparing for war. And war, even though it was a frequent pastime of humans, wasn't exactly a normal condition. When the war was over, what would these people do? Prepare for another war? Each of them was happy only when engaged in working at his particular trade, Mark had gathered. And most of the trades were connected with the manufacture of war supplies. It appeared that they either had to engage in war activities, or be unhappy. Curiouser and curiouser.

There was something fishy about the whole thing. Men were

*Mark took a quick step forward, and
slapped the gun out of Vargo's hand.*

essentially individuals. Mark doubted if any amount of propa-
ganda would ever change that. And they certainly weren't acting
as individuals when they were willing to wait on a sidewalk for
interminable periods while a stream of trucks sped past and
offered them no chance to cross.

People hadn't acted that way in his day. A twentieth-century pedestrian would fret on a corner waiting for a green light,
and then complain bitterly that nobody was given a fair chance
because the light changed to red again before anyone got further
than the middle of the street. And ten minutes later in his own
car, he would fume at the slow-moving pedestrians who took
too long to get across a street.

Mark knew, or thought he did, that men couldn't help being
self-centered. Man invariably considered his own interests first
and those of the tribe second. The interests of the tribe were
considered first only when they coincided with the interests of
the individual. That had been the keynote of all the speeches of
statesmen and politicians, whether they were running for office

or advocating a policy of statecraft. Before the people would cooperate on a matter of policy they had to be convinced that the policy was to their individual benefit. If they were being incited to war, you had to get them all wrought up about it as individuals before you could get much co-operation from them. Either by arousing their personal indignations or by scaring the pants off them.

Omega had once said sarcastically that man was always in a fever to give others the benefit of his own superior well-being. But that had, of course, been only sarcasm. For wars had always been fought because somebody thought he saw a chance of getting something.

Yet this projected war seemed to be different. The young soldier he had spoken to hadn't mentioned a thing about personal glory or gain. He had said something about lifting the world from savagery, and the glory of his generation. Nothing personal; an ant might have said the same thing. But men weren't ants. Rats, sometimes, or worms—but not ants.

Vargo seemed to be the seat of the trouble, but Mark didn't intend to be hauled before the king as a prisoner. Not when there were other ways. His inspection of the cell door had revealed the fact that he wasn't a prisoner at all. It was locked, of course, but it just wasn't sufficiently strong to hold him if he didn't want to be held. And Mark had decided that he didn't want to be.

THE DOOR was a lattice-work affair, and it wouldn't be practical to try to make an opening large enough to pass his body through. That would necessitate ripping the thing to pieces, a feat which might have been beyond even his great strength.

Nor could he see the arrangement of the tumblers, and operate them by *telekinesis*. But there was a much simpler system, in the case of this particular door. The latch was of the sliding variety and although he couldn't slide it free of its socket, he could do the next best thing. He grasped the center bar in both hands, placed a foot on each side of the door, and pulled. His

muscles writhed beneath his bronzed skin and bunched themselves in knots.

The door slowly bent in the middle. As it did, the latch slid
out of its socket. In a few seconds he was free. Mark had always
been athletic and strong, but he never could have done *that*,
in the old days, before he'd taken Omega's mental course in
muscle-building.

He stepped swiftly down the corridor, looking in all the cells
until he came to the elderly Dodd. The old man was seated on a
bench, sobbing softly, his face buried in his hands.

"Take it easy, pop," Mark advised. "All is not as bad as it
seems."

Dodd looked up incredulously, blinking his eyes. "Are you a
man or a god?" he gasped.

"Man, mostly," chuckled Mark, applying himself to Dodd's
cell door. "Me, Tarzan," he grunted and thumped himself on the
chest. Dodd obviously thought he was crazy. "*Sic transit* Weiss-
muller," Mark murmured and got back to work on the door.

The old man, muttered to himself as he saw the door bend
gradually outward until it no longer was locked. Mark didn't
hear the words but he gathered that Dodd had already deified
him. He found that apotheosis no longer embarrassed him. The
Norse had done it too when they had seen his extra-human
abilities. If he explained to people about Omega, and about
his radio-active blood and its properties, nobody would understand, and he'd find himself deified anyway. And it made little
difference, anyhow.

Men either worshiped him or fought him, for one reason or
another.

"Do you have any place to go where you'll be safe?" he asked
the old man. "Somewhere that you can hide for a few days?"

Dodd looked at him uncomprehendingly for a moment, then
nodded. Mark led him down the corridor to the door through
which they had entered.

"The driveway is only a few feet from the sidewalk," Mark

reminded him. "Just walk out naturally and nobody will notice you. Don't run or attract any attention. Good luck."

Mark waited until the old man was safely away and then strode down the corridor to the door at the other end. For an instant he hesitated; then, just to reassure himself, he levitated to the ceiling and down again to the floor. Satisfied, he flung the door open to confront four guards, only just more surprised than he. He really hadn't expected to see anyone behind that door, for he had heard no voices through it. "Soundproof, huh?" Mark said.

Surprised as they must have been, the guards' actions were automatic. With scarcely any hesitation they all drew their pistols.

"Put those things down!" yelled Mark. "They'll bite you!"

Their gun butts began to wiggle in their hands. They gawped in amazement, did a spontaneous quartet in high B-flat, and hurled their weapons down. "Jeeps, snakes!" said one.

Mark wondered idly if a bite from one of the four vipers that the men were convinced they saw, could harm them to any extent. He concluded that it probably would, for hypnotic suggestion is a powerful agent.

Next time he'd use something else. Fuzzy caterpillars would be nice.

"BUNCH OF snake-charmers, eh? Very nice," he remarked. "Where can I find Vargo? I'm tired of waiting."

One of the guards pointed shakily through a window, before he remembered that Mark was supposed to be a prisoner and that the drinks were definitely not on the house.

Glancing through the window, Mark saw, across a greenly wooded square, portions of what seemed to be a very ornate and pretentious mansion. Vargo's palace, without a doubt.

He turned to the guards, who were recovering from their awe at the peculiar activities of their guns, and fixed them with eyes gleaming faintly with amusement.

"When was I to be taken before Vargo?"

Eyes a-popping, one of the men managed to stammer something intelligible. "Tomorrow morning, when he stands trial over those who would hamper the progress of our great city."

"What is he doing now?"

"He confers with the ancestors at this hour, in his palace."

"*Those* are the lads I want to have a look at."

Mark left by way of the front entrance and crossed the street toward the iron fence which enclosed the palace grounds. The four guards would awaken in a few minutes utterly devoid of any memory of either Mark or Dodd. Happily, they would also forget about their guns.

"No sense climbing," Mark said and called on his newly-gained talent. Somewhat awkwardly, he floated over the iron fence. Then with more assurance, he soared rapidly toward the palace. This, he reflected, was much better than walking, and decidedly more impressive. At the moment it was the latter that counted. Vargo must be impressed. Mark didn't enjoy being arrested every time he turned around; made a prisoner at every turn, and he certainly didn't intend to waste time by going through the normal but probably complicated procedure to obtain audience with the king.

At the outer door stood two guards, each with a long rifle in addition to his side arms. At the sight of Mark, speeding toward them with his feet elevated a full foot from the ground, each leveled his rifle and fired. It came so suddenly that Mark was almost caught off guard.

He had expected anyone who saw him to be so astounded at his spectacular form of locomotion that he would be momentarily paralyzed. But not these two.

They acted quite as quickly, and with as few signs of awe, as if he had come up on roller skates. He had barely time to act before the rifles rang out sharply, and the singing bullets whined just beneath his feet. Mark had moved upward.

The guards didn't get another chance to fire. Omega had

developed Mark's hypnotic ability to the *nth* degree—to a far greater power than could possibly have been developed in the lifetime of a normal human. Furthermore Omega had wanted Mark to use that ability, saying if he didn't keep in practice, he'd never get ahead. And Mark, at last, had decided to forget his outmoded ideas about fair play. After all you wouldn't hesitate to use a gun on a savage who was attacking you, even if he did have only a club, Mark reasoned. So he eyed the guards firmly.

Mark descended to the ground before them. He looked deeply into the eyes of one of the rigid soldiers, and made a vigorous effort to probe his brain. Nothing. Mark frowned and tried the other. Nothing there either. Mark was both annoyed and baffled. It was his first attempt at this sort of thing, and it took him quite a while to establish the necessary contact with the sleeping brain. When he finally did, it all came in a rush; and Mark was really surprised at what he found.

"Nasty," he said. "Very nasty indeed."

FOR THE deeper he probed into the man's brain the more astonished he became. The man's training had been of the best. His morals were good and his ideals were admirable. He knew and practiced the golden rule as much as a human being can and stay human.

Yet he firmly believed that it was noble to go out and slaughter any chance person who should resist the spread of Detroit's magnificent civilization. Furthermore he could see no wrong in instantly shooting anybody who happened to come into the enclosure which surrounded the palace. For such had been the orders of Vargo, Giver of Life.

He was to ask no questions, just shoot on sight anybody who tried to get in, except at certain specified hours. The fact that Vargo had ordered it, made it a sublime duty, and not subject to rationalization.

There were other beliefs locked in that brain which were totally at variance with the man's basic character. Mark saw the answer, even though the man had no conscious knowledge of why he reacted the way he did. Vargo was the hypnotist who had planted those pernicious ideas. And Mark suddenly realized what Omega had discovered. He knew now why the people of Detroit were so satisfied with Vargo and his reign. They had all been hypnotized!

Mark shuddered inwardly. Now he knew what was in the back of Dodd's mind when he claimed that the old men were the only sane ones in the city. They had been well along in years when Vargo had started his campaign, and possibly because they lacked usefulness, had escaped Vargo's eye. And Dodd probably suspected the truth.

"Oh, nasty," Mark said again, genuinely shocked.

With the realization of what had been going on, Mark saw the wisdom of Omega's stand on hypnotism. If everyone developed and used his latent power in this direction, a man like Vargo would never be able to get away with it. For a hypnotist can do nothing against a strongly opposing will. And the will is like the muscles—it must be developed and trained. Vargo was a mental muscleman, a gangster of the brain, a freak intellectual giant. And unfortunately Vargo was a freak in other ways. He was an ego-maniac who had no respect for others, thinking only of satisfying his own personal passion for power.

Vargo, he decided, would take a spot of looking into. "Take me to Vargo!" he commanded the two soldiers.

CHAPTER VIII

VARGO SAYS, "THUMBS DOWN!"

THEY OBEDIENTLY FELL into step beside him as he floated through the doorway. Once inside, Mark let them precede him. They crossed a garishly decorated reception hall and stopped before two bronze doors set in an archway. And Mark knew why.

A post-hypnotic suggestion of Vargo's was working, forbidding them to enter. Mark erased the suggestion and the men pushed the doors open. Evidently Vargo had considered it unnecessary to protect himself with locked doors. He had adequate protection planted in the minds of those about him. But he hadn't foreseen a more powerful mind than his countermanding his orders.

To Mark, who had spent the last twelve years in the frugal surroundings of the Vikings, the room which he entered was awe-inspiring. High and domed with varicolored glass it was of dimensions to stagger the imagination.

The floor was of marble tile arranged in intricate designs. In the exact center of the room was a raised dais, surrounded by a curved wall of thick glass. Behind the glass were six chairs, apparently cast of solid gold, and beautifully chased. Seated in the chairs were six men as gaudily clothed as a technicolor version of Roman sybarites.

Mark, wincing a little, nevertheless advanced as calmly as if he had spent his whole life in just such a place as this. He reminded himself that he had come to impress, not to be impressed.

The six men noted his presence at once and turned to face him. They also were obviously determined not to be surprised. But the man in the largest and centermost of the chairs, seemed to be suffering from another emotion. His lined and evil countenance showed plainly that he was livid with rage. And no wonder, Mark reflected. Here Mark was—a forbidden intruder, ushered in by two of Vargo's own guards, both of whom should have found it impossible to enter this chamber, let alone to bring along a friend, and one who was floating through the air at that.

Vargo's rage subsided suddenly, and was replaced by a vague fear.

Mark stopped at the edge of the glass enclosure and turned to the soldiers. "Resume your posts and forget that you ever saw me. When you get to the outside door your minds will be free." He realized he was sounding like a road company of *Frankenstein,* but it couldn't be helped.

The guards obeyed, closed the bronze doors as they left the chamber. Six men scowled at him through the glass as Mark faced them. Vargo fought down his apprehension and returned to normal, and Vargo's normal was something to behold.

"Who are you?" he roared, his face darkened in rage.

"I'll be right with you." Mark grinned charmingly, and rose in the air, passing over the glass barrier. He descended, facing the six seated men. For a moment, at the top of his rise, he hadn't been quite sure he'd get down again, but he negotiated the descent successfully. Even with a certain distinction.

"You're Vargo, I suppose," he said to the oldest of the six.

"Vargo, Giver of Life! And bow when you speak to me!"

Mark laughed. "Don't," he said, "be stuffy. I'm Mark, Protector of the Planet, and Messenger of Omega, the Omnipotent—since we're dealing in titles. Of course they're homemade—like yours."

Vargo's rage was obviously strangling him. His face took on the purplish tinge of gradual asphyxiation. "Why are you here?" he choked.

"Omega sent me," Mark explained. "He doesn't seem to think highly of your system of government. Neither do I, for that matter. And neither of us likes war. So you'll have to give up the whole idea, I'm afraid. Sorry, but there it is."

VARGO'S RAGE suddenly seemed to evaporate; he became almost benign in aspect. The change set off a little alarm in Mark's brain and sent him zooming upward just as Vargo calmly drew his gun and placed a bullet through the spot where Mark had recently been. Mark was about to descend on the old man and disarm him before he could correct his aim, but Vargo just as calmly replaced the pistol in its holster.

Mark came to rest on the floor a little closer to Vargo than he had been before. Another such attempt would find him prepared to strike back.

"Target practice?" he inquired.

"For a minute I thought…" Vargo muttered half under his breath, then answered aloud. "No protection against bullets, eh? You have to dodge." Then suddenly the rage returned, but this time directed against his five companions. "Incompetents!" he roared. "Why haven't you given it to me? My books say that the ancients had it. And here is a modern man with the power. Dolts!"

Mark was somewhat surprised when the five turned their scowls on Vargo. He realized that they had been scowling continuously since he first saw them. Yet as he looked at their faces he could easily see that without the scowls they would all have been fine-looking men. Intelligent faces, too—nothing like the evil, pinched countenance of Vargo.

"The power lies within a man," snapped one of them. "We can't give it to you. We don't have it ourselves."

Abruptly Vargo turned toward Mark and drew his gun again.

Mark was capable of movement that seemed merely a blur to the eyes of the five who watched, and the edge of his hand struck the skinny wrist such a violent blow that the bone snapped. Vargo cringed in his chair, holding the wrist.

"Stop playing with that, will you?" Mark stormed, deeply annoyed.

"Kill him!" Vargo yelled. "No man can be stronger than Vargo!"

Mark stepped back a pace expecting a concerted attack from the five, but it didn't come. In unison all five turned their heads away from Vargo.

"You forgot to make that hypnotic," one of them reminded him.

Vargo emitted a hoarse scream of frustration, and twisted in his chair. Too late, Mark saw that Vargo had brought his left hand down on a knob in the design of the right arm of the chair. Immediately a raucous siren sounded which echoed and re-echoed from the walls of the room.

Mark felt the impact of the old man's eyes. "You'll kill yourself!" came his grating voice. "Pick up that gun and blow out your brains!"

So unexpected was the attack that Mark felt himself sinking. The sound of the alarm siren had thrown him off guard and Vargo's hypnotic wave beat into his brain like a trip-hammer. A wave of darkness swept over his consciousness, and he felt himself bending over—groping for the gun!

CHAPTER IX

CHECK YOUR HELMET HERO

THE WAVE BECAME more intense as he marshaled all his strength to resist. The old man *couldn't* beat him down. Omega had said that no human ever possessed as much hypnotic power as he had given Mark. But the hand still reached out gropingly.

Dimly in his ears whined the sound of the siren. Possibly it was the very urgency of the sound, or perhaps it was due to a slight weakening of Vargo's hypnosis wave, that Mark abruptly experienced a lightening in the pall of darkness which was enveloping his mind.

The battle was won.

Mark knew it as certainly as if it were already over. For Mark's power couldn't wane. The same radioactive element which constantly fed his body was also refreshing his brain.

And the longer Vargo strained, the weaker he became. It was only a matter of time.

Mark's hand ceased to grope for the gun, and he gradually straightened. Abruptly the darkness faded and he looked into the weary and beaten eyes of the aged Vargo. But was there....

There was! Mark wheeled and looked through the glass enclosure. Then he knew the reason for the faint look of triumph in Vargo's eyes. The old man had accomplished his purpose! He had held Mark for the minute that it had taken the palace guards to converge on this room in answer to the alarm. Already doors were opening on all sides. Armed men were pouring through them.

Mark knew that now was no time to hang idly around. He would have liked to stay and lock horns once more with Vargo, but it was too late for that.

Vargo's face was horribly distorted, both from pain and from returning rage, as Mark rose swiftly and circled within the huge glass dome overhead. The other five looked upward with mingled expressions of hope and incredulity on their faces.

Vargo pointed with his uninjured arm and screamed orders to the soldiers who were flooding the vast chamber.

To Mark, circling erratically with sudden darts and swoops, they looked like toys, so high was the dome.

Mark was getting a little nervous. What he had counted on to aid his escape wasn't going to happen. Once more Vargo had outwitted him.

Vainly he swept his gaze from one doorway to another, but none of them was left clear of soldiers. He had headed for the dome, figuring that all the guards would congregate beneath him, in the center of the room, and try to shoot him down. That would leave the doors unguarded, and he had intended, the instant one of them was clear, to swoop over the heads of those below and make his escape.

If the plan had worked none of the men below would have been close enough for an accurate shot at his speeding form.

BUT VARGO had foreseen this move and screamed to his men to deploy in a wide-flung, curved line. Some of them he placed at each door, blocking Mark effectively. The rest, by reason of their curved formation, could shoot at Mark from all sides.

"Oh-oh," said Mark. "What do I do now?"

There was one chance, and Mark took it. Pausing momentarily, he invited a volley of shots. They came, almost before he could dart out of the way. About a hundred high-powered bullets struck within a foot of his body.

Chips of green glass rained down into the enclosed circle he had recently quitted. The bullets, which had hit the glass directly, went clear through the thick dome. Shafts of golden sunlight came through the holes.

Occasional bullets struck near Mark's darting figure, but the men below were evidently having trouble focusing on him, with a background of vivid, ever-changing colors to dazzle their eyes.

The glass was set in squares about two feet across, and made a very pretty pattern, but to follow Mark's movements the guards' eyes were forced to shift from one color to another so quickly that the result was a blur which made him practically invisible. Except when he changed direction abruptly, causing a slight pause which gave them an instant in which to fire at him. At these times a lethal hail would surround him.

Apparently none of them noticed that he seemed to pause several times at one particular spot.

Vargo and his five, companions were too busy protecting themselves from the falling glass to notice anything. Vargo, Mark noted in passing, had a very fair vocabulary. With the fifth volley, a great light descended upon them all—informative as well as illuminating. With it came the fragments of the green square. It had parted company from the surrounding squares.

Vargo screamed futilely as he realized what had happened. An echoing yell went up from the soldiers, who briefly saw Mark catapult through the opening he had trapped them into creating. "Thanks, boys," he shouted, as he passed through.

MARK WAS inwardly raging as he sped away from the palace. He had certainly not distinguished himself. Instead of palavering with Vargo he should have immediately subjected him to a dose of hypnosis. He could have placed suggestions in his mind which would have led to better government in the city of Detroit, and the abandonment of the war plans. He could have erased all memory of the intended plans, or better still have placed an active remorse in the old man's mind which would have caused him to exert all his energy toward correcting his mistakes.

That would have been the simplest solution to the whole

problem, for it wouldn't have changed the *status quo* in the least. Any alternate method promised to bring an upheaval which would wreck the city's social and economic system.

Mark cursed himself for the stupidity that had prevented him from thinking of all that sooner. He hoped Omega wasn't in the offing. His last words had been to beware of Vargo. And a little before that, he had dwelt upon the advisability of using every weapon Mark had against an enemy, on the grounds that to do otherwise would prolong the battle.

If Mark had doubted the wisdom of such a procedure, he had ample proof of it now. A battle which might have now been won, was only started.

But Mark had one consolation. He had learned something from his enemy. He knew that Vargo was the hypnotist who had enslaved the population of Detroit. Before, he had only guessed, with the reservation that perhaps one of the Ancestors had been the guilty man. He also knew now that the Ancestors were ordinary men, technicians perhaps, but nothing more. And he half guessed that maybe they weren't entirely in love with the old devil.

From what he had seen and heard, he had deduced that the Ancestors were more or less free mentalities. And it had appeared that they bucked Vargo's will at every opportunity.

Their refusal to shoot him had indicated that. But Vargo didn't seem the type to put up with such opposition as a regular thing. There might have been an altercation before he arrived, and the Ancestors might have been sulky as a result of it.

Mark couldn't forget that Dodd had said that they had part in planning the conquest of the world. Though Dodd, of course, was an old man, full of prejudices and not in possession of all the facts.

Mark's own impression of the Ancestors had been favorable. But that was a problem to be solved later, and perhaps turned to useful account.

Considering everything, he had made a very poor showing.

Now Vargo would be on guard. He would surround himself with a guard that Mark wouldn't be able to penetrate. Mark wouldn't get another chance to use his hypnotic ability. That was certain.

Mark's anger and sense of frustration evaporated slowly, though steadily, as he began to revel in the novel exhilaration of sailing through the air under his own power. This was, without doubt, a distinctly superior means of travel.

Mark could sense all about him the waves of raw energy. It was like moving in a world of liquid—a liquid which offered no resistance to his passage, but instead bore him with resistless force at his slightest whim. A mere thought was all that was needed to direct this force.

As he moved, tentatively changing direction from time to time, he became aware of some of the mechanics of the phenomenon. When he directed his body to move in any certain direction, the waves seemed to bunch behind him, shoving him along at a speed commensurate with the intensity of his mental desire for motion.

Yet there was no feeling of pressure, for the liquid texture of the waves in front of him diminished in proportion to the increase in the opposite direction. When he desired to stop, however abruptly—and he had been pretty sudden about his stops inside the palace dome—the waves bunched up in the direction he had been traveling, effectively halting his flight. Yet there was no body-wrenching jolt, no dizzying rush of blood. It seemed as if the waves were acting equally upon every particle of his body, nullifying the inertia of his motion.

THERE WAS only the whipping, lashing cut of the wind to take some of the pleasure out of flying. Mark remembered how Omega had solved this problem, and decided to try it himself. All that was necessary was to include a portion of the surrounding atmosphere in the motion he was controlling. This would cushion the rush of the outer air so that it wouldn't strike his body.

But simple as that seemed, Mark had left the walls of Detroit far behind by the time he mastered the technique.

In the short few hours since he had acquired his telekinetic power, Mark had only used the waves to move his own body. It required special mental gymnastics to impart motion to foreign bodies.

For quite a while the thing eluded him, but eventually he got it. A few minutes' practice made him quite proficient. The sensation was something like concentrating on two subjects at the same time, but in a little while he was able to ignore the surrounding shell of air and think of nothing but his own motion. He knew, by the decreasing amount of mental effort required to fly, that it wouldn't be long before he would be able to ignore that too.

It would become as natural as walking—an automatic mechanical action, requiring no conscious supervision.

Idly, as he changed direction to head back toward the city, he wondered if he would ever be able to do the things with telekinesis that Omega could. The quickness with which he mastered control of a body of moving air told him that he might go a long way in that direction, if not actually achieve virtual mastery. His new sense and its mechanical adaptations were becoming more a part of him as each minute went by.

The human brain, he knew, was a versatile entity. It could control innumerable mechanical activities without supervision. Dozens of involuntary bodily functions went on without any consciousness on the part of the individual.

The brain also was capable of controlling several independent voluntary actions simultaneously as well. A man, for instance, could walk down a street, read a book, listen for sounds of approaching vehicles, hum a tune, and perhaps scratch a mosquito bite—and at the same time be hazily conscious of an offending horn and the sounds, floating through a nearby window, of Mrs. Murphy's timely remarks anent the current condition of Mr. Murphy.

Possibly then, a human brain would be capable, with sufficient practice, of emulating the feats of the redoubtable Omega. Mark might some day be able to direct these waves he could now feel so that they would be transformed into matter. *That* would be an accomplishment.

He could picture himself handing Nona a pair of platinum bracelets, beautifully wrought and studded with diamonds, and saying nonchalantly: "Just something I dreamed up while I was shooting a game of pool with the boys."

On the other hand, Mark suddenly realized, even if he did learn to transform the energy of the waves into matter, it would still be necessary to construct matter in the forms that nature had constructed it. Anything less would be unstable and would certainly fly apart instantly. Atomic structure would have to be faithfully reproduced, and that necessitated a thorough knowledge of the exact nature of the matter to be formed.

If he could have looked into the future, back in those days in the twentieth century when he picked the profession he was to study, he would most certainly have majored in physics rather than radio engineering. Instead of allowing radio to become his ruling passion, he would have spent all his time getting a vivid mental picture of the atomic set-up of the various elements.

The platinum bracelets, beautifully wrought and studded with diamonds, would have to wait for a while. At the present state of Mark's knowledge of atomic structure they might turn Nona's arms green. She wouldn't like that.

THE SIGHT of the city once again speeding past beneath him brought Mark back to a realization of his present problems. The city, inhabited for the most part by happy, industrious people, was soon going to be a vast army intent upon conquering the rest of the world. And those very people would be decimated in the process. Yet they were all in favor of setting upon the mad project.

He doubted if any of them—with the possible exception of the caravan guards—knew what they were going to run into.

He doubted if Vargo himself could envision the results of such
a campaign; the slaughter it would involve; and the inevitable starvation and pestilence which would follow. No, Vargo
couldn't know.

There had been no large-scale war on the earth since the last
one almost six thousand years ago. Vargo didn't even know the
elements which go to make up an efficient military organization. The Ancestors, however, were well aware of the horrors of
war. But had they told Vargo? Did they *want* him to go blindly
ahead, hoping that the attempt would end in failure, and that
the people would depose or kill him? Or were they just waiting
for old age to put an end to his activities?

But, Mark might be wrong in his impressions. The Ancestors
might actually be aiding and abetting Vargo of their own free
will. He hoped that wasn't the answer.

The sun was still some distance from the horizon, and Mark
decided that it wouldn't do to descend to the street level by his
present means of travel. The first time he had caused enough
commotion to last him for a while. He landed on a tall building
and found an entrance on the roof. It led him down a stairway
to the top floor, and from there he took an elevator to the street.

He emerged from the building boldly counting upon being
mistaken for one of the thousands of citizens who were being
recruited for the army. His soft doeskin trunks were near enough
to the regulation trunks of the soldiers; and his belt, though now
weaponless, was similar to theirs. And many of the men he had
seen were also without weapons.

He had taken about ten steps away from the doorway of the
building when he was reminded that he had forgotten something.

A policeman was approaching, coming directly toward him.
At first he didn't seem to pay any particular attention to Mark,
then his eyes lifted to the winged helmet. Mark saw his expression change, and instantly knew the answer.

Vargo had broadcast an alarm for him and with it, a description of the helmet!

CHAPTER X

LADY IN MID-AIR

NONA WAS TRYING hard to keep so busy that she wouldn't have time to miss Mark. She had just completed a curriculum for older children, and was planning to set out for the king's castle to get his signature to authorize its use.

She would arrive just after he completed his afternoon meal. Then she'd convince him that her new curriculum was just the thing. That wouldn't be hard, of course, for the king invariably authorized anything either Mark or she recommended.

He was just as superstitious as his subjects and was fully convinced of Mark's relationship to the Norsemen's galaxy of gods. Nona also was considered somewhat removed from common mortals, if for no other reason than the fact that she was Mark's mate.

The king heartily approved of her school projects, though he would have sanctioned them even if he hadn't. Nevertheless Nona combed and fussed and primped just as if she weren't at all sure of her success. That, if anyone had given it a thought, would have been sufficient to indicate that Nona was all human—and all woman.

Not that any great amount of evidence was needed to prove it. For Nona possessed the same radioactive blood that made Mark impervious to Norwegian temperatures; and she refused to wear any more clothes than a decent minimum. Summer and winter her costumes were brief and designed for utility rather than warmth. And utility with Nona meant freedom of movement. Mark's tendency to while away hours at the sport of sham axe-fighting, and his insistence upon using her for a sparring partner, required that she forego the frills which usually accompany feminine attire.

In spite of the utilitarian nature of her raiment, however, there was nothing institutional-looking about it. Nona smiled at herself in her full-length mirror, quite satisfied with the effect. Her reflection dutifully smiled back. It was a nice smile, one of the several items which usually kept Mark from cavorting all over the globe on epic errands.

Above the smile was a pert nose and a pair of level, but impish eyes. Below the smile came a firm chin, and beneath that, the virtually invisible costume, consisting mainly of a gaily colored jacket which fell just short of reaching the top of a narrow, flared skirt, which in turn decidedly did not come even close to tripping her. A pair of soft, leather sandals completed the outfit, but they seldom, if ever, were noticed.

It was while thus occupied, and mentally going over the things she was going to say to the king, that she was startled to hear the outer door burst inward with a clatter. It banged back against the wall and was followed by the sound of light, quick footsteps.

Nona's smile changed and she waited to see what would happen next. Mark was the only one who opened a door like that. It was the one thing that he never did quietly. His fist, popping open the door, always announced his approach. But Mark had sailed for America three days ago.

YET... HER boudoir door banged open with the same explosive suddenness and there stood Mark, arms outstretched. Nona rushed to his arms with a cry of delight. "Darling—oh, Mark, you're back." She kissed him fervently, and then drew back questioningly.

"What are you doing here?" she cried. "You're supposed to be on your way to Detroit."

"Changed my mind," he answered. "Told Omega off—and

came back." He kissed her again, and this time she responded with less vigor.

Nona disengaged herself from his arms and stood back a pace, looking at him absorbedly. "Kiss me again, please." He obeyed. "I thought so." She smiled very sweetly. "I want you to do something for me, sugar-pie," she said in tones of honey. "I want you to turn around the other way. Face the door."

Mark did, puzzled. Whereupon Nona planted an emphatic kick on the seat of his doeskin trunks. "Omega—you devil!" Nona said, furiously. He lifted a full foot off the floor, turning around to face her before again touching the floor. When he did, he was no longer Mark, but a weazened old gent with a reproachful look on his lined and wrinkled face. His eyes were slightly askew and he rubbed the spot where Nona's sandal had contacted his spurious anatomy.

"I wouldn't do that to you," he complained.

"You deserve a good deal worse. No—really—of all the nasty tricks! You ought to be ashamed."

"I just wanted to check up and see if I was missing anything," Omega said. "How's the kids?"

"You're a lecherous old man, and I should be furious."

Nona seemed to be slightly mollified at his inquiry. "They're both at school. They're wonderful. I'm really prouder of them than I can—"

Omega made a deprecating gesture. "No need to be proud," he claimed. "After you've taught them all you know, they'll still be a couple of nitwits."

Nona glared angrily and reached for a heavy wrought-brass candlestick. Omega promptly disappeared and then reappeared in a somewhat disturbing form, resembling something between a spider and an octopus, with most of the uglier features of both. With a span of about four feet, his eight hairy legs supported a globular body from which sprouted six writhing tentacles. A black, chitinous armour protected the body. "Take that thing off and put on something human, you old goat. You know it makes me ill. I don't care if you did say it was your original body, and considered quite beautiful in certain demented circles."

Those circles had existed in the days when the Earth's satellite was inhabited by similar creatures, and Omega, once he had discovered Nona's distaste for it, invariably reassumed the form whenever he considered that she had outraged his peculiar idea of dignity.

"I don't believe it, anyway. Nothing ever looked like that. It's disgusting... Where is Mark? Have you seen him?"

"Sure, I saw him. Didn't I tell you?"

"No. You were too busy trying to find out if you'd been missing anything. How is he?"

"Okay, I guess. Got himself tangled in another war, but don't worry about that. He'll come out all right."

Nona placed her hands on her hips. "I don't suppose *you'd* have any idea how he came to be involved in this war, would you?

Omega went back to being an old man again and his aged countenance took on a sheepish look, albeit the eyes were twinkling. "It's his job, you know," he said. "I just happened to notice a condition which needs correction, so I dropped in on him while he was out in the middle of the Atlantic Ocean. As soon as I told him what was what, he was all of a dither to get to work."

"Where is he now?" Nona demanded.

"A place called Detroit. He's having all kinds of fun."

"*All* kinds... This needs looking into. Take me to Detroit!"

Omega smiled indulgently. "Are you sure you really want to go? How about the children?"

"You just want to argue," she accused. "The children will be perfectly all right. Better than you'll be if you don't take me to Mark!"

"Well... All right. But don't blame me if you don't like it."

NONA HAD no time to think about whys and wherefores before she found herself flying through the air; high above the vast Atlantic. She didn't know it, but Omega had visited her for the very purpose of transporting her to America. Having some faint knowledge of the workings of the female mind, he had thought it best to have her make the suggestion. He congratulated himself on a masterful job of conniving.

"I want to teach you something," remarked Omega. "I think you're going to do quite a bit of traveling this way in the future, if you intend to keep up with Mark, and at the same time keep in touch with your kids."

Nona took the cryptic statement at its face value, not suspecting that Omega was glancing into the future and solving some problems that hadn't come up yet. Accordingly there was nothing to distract her mind as Omega excited that portion of her brain which enabled her to sense the liquid waves of energy which surrounded her.

Nona's mind was fairly well conditioned by twelve years of intermittent contact with the disembodied intelligence, and quite prepared to take in her stride anything that he might do. Experience had taught her that he was totally unpredictable, and never to be surprised at anything.

By the time the shoreline of America's Atlantic coast slid beneath them, Nona was traveling under her own power. She was doing more than that, for Nona's temperament was such that she applied herself assiduously to anything which would make her a better companion to Mark.

In less than an hour she was controlling a body of air which traveled with her and shielded her from the blast of wind caused by her swift flight. Furthermore she was describing all sorts of maneuvers and aerial evolutions, which made Omega extend himself to keep pace. For Omega was not the only one who earned the name of being unpredictable. With no notice at all Nona would suddenly stop and speed off at right-angles to their course, then drop suddenly until she skimmed the tree-tops, and resume the proper direction.

Omega became a little weary of following her erratic course. "You seem to be pretty proficient," he observed. "So I'll go about my business. Cross this lake and then the next. Follow the river at the end of the second lake. On the left bank you will find Detroit. So long!"

"But how will I find Mark? Don't go...."

Nona found herself conversing with thin air, and gave up. She suddenly felt all alone and slightly scared. At the moment she was soaring at a height of several thousand feet. Clouds were beneath her and all sight of the earth was cut off.

Panic momentarily claimed her. She suddenly felt a rush of wind. The enclosing body of air had vanished! Not realizing what had happened—that in her turbulent mental state she had forgotten to keep control over the moving atmosphere—she lost what vestige of calmness she still possessed.

For several seconds she tried to gain control of her emotions as the biting wind whipped and tore at her inky hair. Then she suddenly realized that she was falling! Clouds which had been below her were now surrounding her, damp foggy mist shutting out all vision.

CHAPTER XI

NO SLAVES ARE WE

IN THE COURSE of a split second, during which the policeman revealed by his expression that he recognized him as a wanted man, Mark's mind raced through several thoughts and reached a conclusion. The helmet, of course, had caused the expression. Which meant that Vargo had broadcast an alarm, describing it as an outstanding means of identification.

Further, Vargo feared him, and knew him to be a master hypnotist. Then, he wouldn't order him captured, for Vargo knew that he would be able to hypnotize anybody who tried it, and an attempt would only put Mark on his guard. Therefore, he would order Mark shot on sight.

But Vargo had reckoned without Mark's quick mental processes. Before the cop's mind was able to accept the evidence of his eyes and act upon it, Mark was ready for action. The officer's hand streaked toward his pistol, then froze. For an instant it hovered above the butt of the gun. Then it descended and grasped the gun, pulling it from its holster—and handed it, butt foremost to Mark.

"Better unfasten that holster, too," directed Mark, accepting the gun. "You won't need it."

The man obeyed while Mark took off his helmet and considered the advisability of swapping with the cop. But that would be a dirty trick. The first policeman who saw it would take a pot-shot at the man who wore it. He compared it with the helmet of the cop and noticed that if it weren't for the wings, the two were almost identical. That solved the problem. He would wrench off the wings, put them in his belt pouch, and have them welded on again after this business was settled.

He gave one of them a twist and was surprised to have it turn in his hand, instead of breaking off. The things had been screwed on. Quite pleased with this discovery, he unscrewed both wings and placed them in his pouch.

The officer's short-sword followed, fitting the strap which had held his axe. Then Mark fastened on the proffered holster and put the gun in it. A careful check revealed the fact that except for several inches of superior height, he now looked approximately as the cop had looked a minute before.

Passersby might have wondered momentarily at the exchange, but so hectic were the times, with all their fevered preparation for war, that anything might have a logical explanation. There was certainly nothing indicating an unfriendly attitude between the two men.

And in a minute the shorter man said a cheerful goodbye to the taller one, and ambled off down the street. An observer couldn't possibly guess that the taller of the two had just given an hypnotic command for the shorter one to forget the whole matter and go about his business.

Nor could it be guessed that the shorter man would soon miss his weapons and blame the theft on a practical joke of one of his associates. Nor that he would quietly filch a new set of equipment from the police armory, and keep the incident to himself.

MARK STRODE off in an opposite direction, feeling for the moment quite pleased with himself. That, however, lasted for only a block or so. Then his mind became filled with the problem of what to do with Detroit. And that turned out to be quite a problem.

He attacked it from several angles.

His final idea on the subject was that he'd better not try to formulate a plan of action until he had learned a few more things about the setup in Detroit. He knew where to gain the information, but he'd have to wait a few hours.

The sun was still visible in the western sky and darkness was necessary before he could act. In the meantime he'd observe as much as possible about the people of the city, and perhaps get a better idea of the things he would have to do to cope with the inevitable economic strife which would result from the abandonment of the war.

His footsteps led him toward the edge of the city; toward that narrow belt which furnished all the growing things needed by its population.

There was a tavern near one of the growth stations. He mingled with some of the workers who were washing down the dust accumulated during the day's work. One of them, who seemed to be well supplied with currency, was glad to foot the bill for Mark's drinks, under the impression that he was an old friend.

Mark used hypnotism to accomplish this end, for two very good reasons. One was that men were a bit more garrulous when in their cups; and another was that he had none of the type of money accepted as legal tender in Detroit.

In the tavern he learned about the ill effects of the growth ray. Two of the men present were continually annoyed by trouble with their "innards," and complained bitterly that they would be able to work several more hours a day if it weren't for the leakage in the vibration machine which was causing the mysterious malady.

But neither held any resentment because his work was slowly killing him. The only complaint was that it kept him away from the machine he loved.

Mark went out of the place fuming, and vowing that something would be done about it, but soon.

He noticed that the sun was gone and the sky was getting darker in the west. Accordingly he set out in a direction calculated to bring him closer to the palace. He had some business to conduct there, but he wanted the night to be well advanced when he arrived. He walked slowly.

For a few blocks Mark's new direction carried him along busy streets, thronged with homeward-bound workers. Detroit was like any large city of his own era, in spite of the peculiarities which made it, unhappily, unique. There were stores, taprooms and amusement houses; congestion, squalor and well-kept parks; in short, everything which went to make up a busy metropolis.

Old, familiar things.

Mark felt himself becoming homesick, but not quite the same way he had felt when he had first looked down on the city from the heights. Now he felt as if he were returning to something he had considered lost, forever.

Hazy ideas were forming in his brain as he watched the hectic activity of the people about him. These were the same sort of people who had inhabited twentieth-century New York, Philadelphia and Chicago. Once delivered from the regimented mental processes imposed by Vargo, they would represent a nucleus which could grow and gradually fill the entire land. America as it was in his own day!

SO ENGROSSED had Mark become in his thoughts that he failed to notice, except vaguely, that the street he was following was less imposing than the main thoroughfare it had been a while before.

Almost aimlessly, as he waited for the night to grow older, he had wandered on beyond the factory and shopping areas and was now in a section of the city which could have stood a good deal of improvement. Squalid tenements now lined the street, few of them lighted with electricity. Oil lamps, here and there, were dimly lighting unwashed windows.

Mark's first knowledge that he had walked out of the more modern portion of the city came with a fetid odor of decaying garbage from a nearby alleyway. Abruptly his brain became conscious of the things that his eyes had been seeing for some time. He frowned, and glanced toward the offending alleyway, which was now only a few feet distant.

The frown changed to sudden astonishment. Standing in the shadow of the opening was a man, pointing an automatic directly at his stomach!

He was a strongly-built young man, dressed as scantily as Mark himself, and was wearing a faintly amused smile. His eyes seemed to twinkle merrily, and that was probably what deterred Mark from instantly driving at him all the power of his hypnosis wave. The man, obviously, had watched him approach and hadn't used his gun. Therefore he didn't intend to use it. Mark was curious, and curiosity had led him into trouble on more than one occasion.

He stopped and waited.

"You certainly were wool-gathering," the man remarked, conversationally. "That's bad in this neighborhood. What's in the pouch?"

Mark grinned, quite pleased. "An old-fashioned holdup! I'm beginning to like this town. Though I can't see how you figure into Vargo's setup. Don't tell me that you're selflessly devoted to being a footpad."

The man's eyes narrowed and the amused look was replaced with one that didn't augur well for anyone who opposed him. "It's my life's work," he replied evenly. "But not because I wish it. Vargo's little Vocation Board made a mistake. But don't try to talk yourself out of anything. I've been in business too long for that. What's in the pouch?"

"Wings," stated Mark. "They go on my hat. I fly with them when I'm in a hurry."

"Interesting. Move your hands slowly and don't go near that gun. Let's see the wings."

Mark did as he was told, removing the wings from the pouch. He showed the holdup artist how they fitted in his helmet. "Made of iron," he said. "They aren't valuable."

"Except for flying, eh?"

Before the man could fire a shot, Mark lifted vertically into the air and sailed over the roof of the building next to the alley. He descended farther back in the alleyway, and swooped down behind the holdup man, pinioning his arms.

In an instant he had disarmed him.

"I don't like people to point guns at me," he said. "What's your name? And get your chin up off your chest. You look like a fish."

The man clicked his jaws shut and recovered from his astonishment in record time. "That was hypnotism," he deduced. "One of Vargo's boys, eh?"

IT WAS Mark's turn to be astonished. Here was a citizen, it seemed, who knew what was going on. Dodd, he remembered, had suspected but wasn't certain. This man knew.

Mark shook his head.

"No," he said. "That wasn't hypnotism. I really flew. And I'm not one of Vargo's boys, as he would be only too glad to tell you. I'm Mark Nevin. I'm a stranger here myself. And no friend of Vargo's. Who are you?"

"Just a thief. Tolon by name," answered the man, suspiciously. "But don't tell me you flew. I know hypnotism when I see it."

Mark scratched his chin and regarded Tolon thoughtfully. He was looking at a rugged, cleanly-chiseled face, not at all the criminal type—if there was such a thing. Tall, almost as tall as himself, the man reminded him of pictures he had seen of the American frontiersman of colonial days. Fine lines at the corners of the eyes spoke of time spent out in the open, as did a tan which almost matched Mark's own. Slightly uptilted lips indicated that his present grim and suspicious expression was not his usual one. Mark decided he liked Tolon, thief or not.

On impulse he handed back the gun, butt foremost.

"Where can we talk?" he asked. "I'm a stranger here, and I want to learn a few things."

Tolon took the pistol, looked at it as if unable to credit his senses, then seemed to make a decision. He beckoned a hand and moved off down the street. Mark followed quickly after.

The way led through a dimly lit section of winding, narrow streets and odorous alleys. It was an older portion of the city, one which would have been impenetrable to the modern trucks which sailed along the wider streets. The journey ended as abruptly as it had begun, when Tolon vanished quickly into a dark areaway beside a dark, three-story, stone tenement. Mark was right on his heels as he ducked into a shadowed doorway.

Tolon stopped in a vestibule until Mark had closed the outer door. Then he opened the inner one. Surprisingly the room within was well lighted. Mark blinked his eyes and tried to get them adjusted to the brilliance. After a minute or two he was able to see. He hadn't moved from his position at the door, for he had instantly sensed that the room was full of men. Tolon had moved quickly away from him, and was now facing him with the others. There were five strangers, all seated, and all covering him with pistols!

Mark appraised them carefully, not saying a word. The men looked him over just as carefully. They were a grim lot, and looked like tough customers. None of them appeared inherently vicious; they looked intelligent, not like criminals at all. Yet he could only assume that he had fallen into a den of thieves.

Tolon had been quite frank about admitting that he was on the wrong side of the law.

"What have we here, Tolon?" asked the man on the extreme right, without taking his eyes or his gun from Mark. He spoke quietly, a soft, assured voice which bespoke confidence and knowledge of his own power. Mark could see that the assurance was well founded, for the man was stocky, and muscular in a dynamic way which indicated both strength and agility. His level eyes revealed an intelligence which was in no way subnormal.

"I don't know, Ira," confessed Tolon. "But it's worth looking into."

HE RELATED the encounter, describing the illusion of flying which he said Mark impressed hypnotically on his mind. He mentioned that Mark had said he was a stranger and wanted to learn something; also that he had returned his gun.

"But you're suspicious," added Ira. "Why? Would one of Vargo's men hand you back a gun to shoot him with?"

"It's possible," defended Tolon. "Vargo's agents are resourceful. He may have wanted me to lead him to the rest of our bunch."

"Which, of course, you did," said Ira. "Has it occurred to you, my dear Tolon, that if the man hypnotized you so easily, then he must be a good deal better than Vargo?"

Tolon nodded, puzzled. "I thought of that," he confessed. "But if he didn't, then I must accept the fact that he flew. I couldn't take any chances. He was too close to home."

Ira nodded, and regarded Mark at length. The others held their peace.

"That's right," said Ira, finally. "We can't take any chances. If he's one of Vargo's men, it would be better if he were a corpse. You're sure you haven't had any giggle-water?"

"One drink," said Tolon, smiling.

"Then, my fine fellow, the man either flew or he's a much better hypnotist than Vargo. The name's Mark, isn't it? Can you help us out, or would you rather we made our minds up without your help?"

Mark grinned. "I'd rather help," he said, rising about a foot off the floor, and hovering there nonchalantly.

Ira's eyebrows raised perceptibly, but he showed no other sign of surprise. The others, however, gasped audibly. Ira rose from his chair and moved around toward Mark's side, being careful not to block the guns of the others. Then he quickly passed a hand beneath Mark's feet, touching them lightly on the soles. He muttered briefly and returned to his seat.

"I'm not so sure that this proves anything, except that the man really can fly," Ira pondered. "If anything it indicates that the man is an agent of Vargo's. This stunt could be something new which the Ancestors have developed."

Mark decided that things were going too slowly. He had some business to attend to this evening, and it was nearly time to start. With an abrupt effort of will he threw at them all the power of his hypnosis wave. For a second he felt a vague resistance, then the men froze into immobility. Their guns were still pointed at Mark's middle, but he knew they were harmless. He strode to Ira and gently removed the finger which was locked in position over the trigger. Then he took the gun and placed it on a table across the room. He repeated the operation with each of them, until there was a pile on the table.

"I'm your friend," he told them. "In the future you will obey any order I choose to give. You will know that I work for your own good. But you will remember nothing of what I have just said."

MARK RELEASED them from his hypnotic influence, watching them carefully as he did so. Their reactions were alike as they regained their senses and realized that they no longer held their guns. They looked at Mark dumbly and wonderingly as he returned the weapons, giving each man the one which he had taken from him. Each placed his automatic in its holster. There was no hesitation about the latter act.

"I see you all catch the point, gentlemen," Mark observed. "If I had wished, you would all be dead, or on your way to Vargo's prison. The fact that you're not proves that I'm no agent of Vargo's. My hypnotic ability—so much greater than his—is the reason why Vargo wants me killed. Now, Tolon, suppose you tell me what you meant by saying that in your case the Vocation Board made a mistake."

"It's the same with all of us," Tolon explained. "I completed my schooling and then went to the Vocation Board to be examined. I was placed in a room full of little-mirrors which revolved and reflected light from an electric bulb. A man asked me some questions about my past. I answered, giving all the details. He talked to me in a soft voice, telling me what a great guy Vargo was, and what a great destiny awaited the people of Detroit. Then he told me I was getting drowsy, and to rest my eyes by watching one of the revolving mirrors.

"I was only a kid at the time, with a certain respect for my elders, and obeyed him. I watched one of the mirrors—but I wasn't drowsy, and I didn't get drowsy. He talked some more on the same subject of Vargo and the great destiny of Detroit—how some day we would march forth and conquer the world, spreading our great civilization and giving its benefits to the benighted peoples of other cities. He also kept telling me that I was going to sleep, so I dropped my eyes, not wanting to make him out a liar.

"Then suddenly he must have decided I had dropped off, for he quit talking for a while. Then he said: 'You will obey implicitly. Your mind belongs to Vargo. Isn't that so?' I kidded him along. 'My mind belongs to Vargo,' I said. Then he told me to wait for further orders, and left me sitting there. I stretched and walked around the room, until I heard someone coming. Then I got back in the chair and stared at the wall.

"The man came in and with him was Vargo. 'He is acquiescent,' the guy told Vargo. 'Should make a good guard. We need a few more.' Then Vargo went to work. He sat in front of me and looked into my eyes. Right then I pretty near did go to sleep. Something hit my brain like a sledgehammer, and kept hitting. And all the time Vargo talked.

"He told me that I was admirably suited to be a caravan guard. That I was to obey orders and always realize that he, Vargo, was the greatest ruler on earth—kind, benevolent, and compassionate. I must always remember that his orders were not to be questioned, for they were for my own good and for the good of civilization."

MARK WINCED. Those lines sounded familiar. He consoled himself with the thought that he really meant it. "I see," he interrupted. "The first man was to soften you up for Vargo. With so many to take care, of, Vargo trained men to help him, to save him own strength. In your case they made a mistake. You must have a natural resistance against hypnotism, or you wouldn't be able to remember anything. They told you to forget, didn't they?"

"Vargo told me," said Tolon. "He said to forget that I had ever seen him, but remember that he was my friend and always to be obeyed. I answered the way I figured he wanted me to. I really believed what he said."

"But you began to think, later. Tell me about it."

"I was turned over to the trainers, who taught me to be a good guard, proficient with the sword and bow. I was also taught to shoot, but told never to mention guns on my travels to other cities. Nor was I ever to mention the other things which the people of Detroit accepted as commonplace, but which were unknown to the rest of the world; electricity, automobiles and the rest of our scientific progress. These were to be saved until the day of the conquest. Then they were to be given to the rest of the world.

"Later, long after I entered service as a caravan guard, I began to see the reason for all that. Guns and motor cars would give us a tremendous advantage over people who knew nothing about them, and had no defense against them. That started me thinking. If Vargo was so big-hearted and really wanted to improve the rest of the world, why didn't he give them electricity and all the other things? You don't have to kill somebody when you want to make a gift.

"I began to picture what would happen in some of the cities I visited. Innocent people, without any malice toward anybody, were going to be slaughtered. And a lot of our own people as well. And in most of the cities we do commerce with, there is no need for it at all.

"Their rulers are benevolent, and the people fairly happy and prosperous. We could give them things, all right, but they are doing perfectly well as it is. The aren't oppressed or mistreated. No need for a war. We could improve their lot with our scientific advancement, but there would be no reason to conquer them in the bargain. The only answer was that Vargo intended to rule. His motives were selfish. And that, of course, started me doubting everything which was believed concerning his high ideals. I reached the conclusion, with my memory of what had happened in the Vocation Board building, that almost everyone in Detroit is a mental slave of Vargo.

"So I decided I didn't want to take Vargo's orders any longer. It's the same with these others. When Vargo's hypnosis didn't quite take, they began to think for themselves, finally winding up as thieves. We refuse to do anything to advance Vargo's interests. But on the other hand, we have to eat."

Mark looked thoughtfully around the room, and liked what he saw on their faces. Footpads they might be, but destroyers of Vargo they might become....

CHAPTER XII

THE GIRL WHO WASN'T HYPNOTIZED

A TERRIFIED SHRIEK welled up in Nona's throat as her falling body burst through the misty lower fringes of the cloud bank. The ground below, shadowy in the early twilight, was rushing at her with awesome speed! It turned and twisted as her body revolved and tumbled through the air.

The shriek, thin and shrill in her ears shocked her to sanity. Abruptly she shook off her panic and concentrated on regaining her awareness of the liquid cosmic waves she had been guiding only a minute before. Instantly she felt them, separate and distinct from the buffeting of the lashing wind. The waves pervaded her being, impinging on sense nerves which had lain dormant since her birth. And with the sensation, the ability to manipulate the waves returned.

Abruptly Nona's wild descent halted. She clothed herself with an enveloping blanket of atmosphere, and continued her journey, protected from the blast caused by her swift movement. That, she vowed, catching her breath, would never happen again.

On her left was a broad lake. She remembered Omega's instructions and followed its shore line. Presently there would be another one, and after that a river. On its left bank was her destination. Slightly alarmed at the darkening ground below her, Nona put on more speed, doubling her former velocity. High in the air it was still light, off in the west, but twilight had spread below. And Nona couldn't know that Detroit was a well-lighted city and would be visible for miles.

Omega hadn't told her anything to warn her of coming events. He had just said that Mark was at a place called Detroit. And while Nona was a well-read young lady, she couldn't possibly know anything of the modern Detroit.

Her native city, Hartford, had preserved much in the way of ancient books and arts, and she knew that Detroit had once been an industrious manufacturing center. But she also knew that Hartford was one of the favored spots on the American continent, in the matter of salvaged remains of the twentieth-century civilization.

Other cities of which she knew, while they had been built on the ruins of older ones, had retained very little of the culture that had flourished before the great war. She naturally assumed that Detroit was like them.

"Detroit," Nona muttered to a passing bird who seemed a little startled to see a human being soaring around in territory he had always considered exclusively avian.

NONA WAS more than surprised when she sighted, dimly in the distance, the lights of the city. Several minutes passed, as she sped closer, before she figured out what they were. Even Hartford had failed to revive the lost knowledge of electricity. Only recently, as a result of Mark's efforts, had she known what a city could look like when lighted by it. And she had never seen Stadtland from a height, as she now saw Detroit. Nor was Stadtland nearly as large.

She was momentarily stumped. How would she ever find Mark, in such a big place, among so many people? Where would she start?

Well, it wouldn't do to drop down in the middle of a thronged and well-lighted street. The obvious thing would be to choose a more secluded spot and proceed from there.

So Nona set herself down in a spot that chanced to be within a quarter mile of the building in which Mark was talking to the self-confessed thieves.

No one saw her and she proceeded casually in a direction

calculated to bring
her out on one of
the more well-
lighted avenues.
There was a street
light at the next
corner—a fitful
carbon-arc lamp
which only served
to make the shad-
ows deeper and
darker at the edges
of the small space
which it illumi-
nated.

A young woman
stood against the
side of a building,
negligently watch-
ing the occasional
passersby. She was
gaudily dressed,
wearing a gown
which covered
her completely,
but neverthe-
less accentuated
her well-rounded
figure. Her face,
which was boldly
attractive, was
resplendently
rouged. She saw
Nona approach,
and her eyes grew
sultry.

"Say, that's not fair!" she exclaimed, gaping at Nona's scanty costume. "Besides, you're liable to get arrested."

Nona was puzzled. "I don't understand," she said. "What's not fair?"

The girl's answer never came. She was just opening her mouth when she suddenly shut it and gasped, her eyes widening at something behind Nona. Nona turned and saw a man approaching, his eyes blazingly intent on the girl. He didn't even seem to see Nona.

"There you are!" he grated. "Loafing again. You won't go out on the main street where you should be. You'd rather stay here— I'll fix you!"

Before the startled Nona saw what was coming, the man struck the girl a vicious blow. Blood trickled from her lips as the girl whimpered and shrank away from an upraised foot.

"I'll fix that pretty face of yours," he raged.

The foot never descended. A whirlwind of motion landed out of nowhere. There was a brief flash of rocklike fists, the thwacks of two exuberant blows, and the man was sprawled on his face.

"Mark! Darling!" the girl cried, in what seemed to be the greatest joy.

Nona stared, aghast, as the girl rose nimbly from the pavement and threw herself at Nona's mate. Oh, it was Mark, all right. The girl kissed him with great violence, while he stood as if frozen. The girl finally disentangled herself, and cast a wild eye on the motionless figure on the sidewalk. Then she grabbed one of Mark's hands and tugged.

"Hurry, darling! We mustn't be here when the big bully comes to."

TOGETHER THEY ran off down the street, Mark casting a sheepish glance to the rear. Nona sped along behind, her eyes glistening with, a terrible, vengeful light. Only three days since Mark had left Stadtland and now—Well, he certainly hadn't wasted much time.

Mark and his little friend came to a halt at a dingy tenement in the middle of a row on the next block. A dark hallway, an even darker flight of stairs, and then the girl opened a door which led into a small apartment. Nona followed, composing a series of devastating remarks. The girl wasn't even aware of her presence. An oil lamp revealed that the place was clean and well cared for. It also revealed that the furniture was shabby and in a lamentable state of preservation.

"He won't come back for a while," the girl breathed. "He'll just go and get drunker. And when he does come home, he won't remember a thing."

Nona kicked the door viciously to behind her. It slammed with a wall-shaking clatter. The girl continued to gaze rapturously into Mark's eyes. Mark seemed to like it, even to the point of ignoring the fuming Nona as he gathered the girl into his arms.

Nona suddenly saw the light. She slumped weakly into an over-upholstered chair and glared at Mark. Then she grabbed a heavy pot, leaped to her feet, and brought it forcibly down on his skull. He released the girl and turned to Nona, frowning.

"I wish you'd quit interfering," he said, with some asperity. "After all, you won't let me experiment on you, you know."

Nona stamped her foot. "It's not fair," she contended. "You shouldn't use Mark's body for your experiments. And besides, do you have to have a witness?"

"This isn't Mark's body," Omega snapped.

"Well, it's a darned unreasonable facsimile," she stormed back. "It's—it's indecent."

Omega grinned. "How was I doing?"

Nona hesitated and fingered a lip judiciously. "You're a little weak in the clinches," she decided. "Mark could teach you a thing or two... But I won't let him. You do your own experimenting!"

While they talked the girl stood idly by, looking at them apathetically. There was no expression whatever on her painted face.

"And you'll never learn anything," Nona said, turning back to the spurious Mark, "by hypnotism. It's not nice, either. Let her go."

Omega looked thoughtfully at the girl. As he did so the solid body which looked like Mark, slowly became vague in outline, shimmered faintly, then solidified again. But it had adopted the shape of the aged sage which Omega used in his calmer earthly moments.

"There's something funny about that girl," he said. "She has a natural resistance against hypnotism. I sensed it back there on the street, and used enough power to do the job. But it took a whole lot more than it does to subjugate the average human mind. I'll bring her to. Let's see... For the sake of her mental stability, I'll just leave her a memory of the two of us knocking out her husband, and of her bringing us here."

Omega sank down in the chair which Nona had just left. His eyes glowed momentarily.

The girl stared. "I'm Gladys. I'm awfully grateful to you two."

"I'm Nona. Was that beast your husband?"

The girl nodded, shamefaced. "The law requires him to support me," she explained. "But he spends all he earns on drink. Then he beats me!"

Nona nodded, sympathetically. "This law—Doesn't it protect you? Can't you appeal to a court and make him behave?"

Gladys slumped dejectedly in a creaky chair. "I daren't," she said. "They'd find that I'm not obedient. And that would give me away. They'd make me go before the Vocation Board again."

NONA LEARNED a lot in the next hour or two. Gladys served a hot drink which resembled something between tea and coffee, a product of the forcing grounds which supplied the city's food. She talked animatedly as she bustled about the small kitchen, preparing the hybrid drink.

Gratitude for the rescue was her topic, until Nona asked pointed questions about things she wanted to know. Omega held his peace, contenting himself with making wry faces after each sip of the steaming drink.

Gladys' story wasn't a pretty one, and before long Nona understood very well why Mark was taking an interest in Detroit. Nona was getting the story from a different angle and learned certain things which hadn't as yet come to Mark's attention.

For women as well as men came under the jurisdiction of the Vocation Board, and they didn't fare nearly as well. Some, of course, were used in industry. There were always certain occupations where women excelled. Few, however, held their positions for many years. When their efficiency fell off in the slightest, they returned to the Vocation Board and were then conditioned for woman's more important task, that of bearing children.

One happy part about the arrangement was in the fact that it was customary to subject both the woman and her assigned mate to the ministrations of the Vocation Board. Both left the place thoroughly convinced that destiny had brought them together. And in both were the mental suggestions which ordinarily led to a lasting devotion. This usually resulted in marital bliss, with little or no friction or discontent.

Usually, but not always. Incompatibility still reared its head. Vargo's assistants took full charge of this phase of conditioning the inhabitants of Detroit. Vargo only exercised his superior hypnotic power where the suggestions of loyalty to himself and his aims were concerned.

The majority of Detroit's women, of course, never were used in the industrial plants. There was no need for so many, and therefore only those with special aptitudes were taken. Others were conditioned for matrimony right away.

There were women of still another class, a small minority, who exercised their own choice in the matter of mating. These were the daughters of officials of the government. The families of nobles retained their rights in this respect, though even they, Gladys suspected, were subject to Vargo's hypnotic power. Their loyalty wouldn't otherwise have been so firm.

"But how can such things exist!" exclaimed Nona. "Why don't the people do something about it?"

"But they don't know it," said Gladys, patiently.

"*You* know it."

Gladys nodded. "They didn't hypnotize me. They only thought they did. And I was afraid to object to the husband they chose for me. They would have found out. And I didn't know what they might do to me if they found that I hadn't gone under their spell. You see I realized that everyone was given the same treatment and that none was aware of it. If any had been, I should have heard of it. Therefore I was afraid to admit that I had resisted."

Nona saw the sense to that. People who ruled by such an expedient would go to great lengths to prevent their methods from becoming known.

"Your husband—"

Gladys nodded. "That's the pitiful part," she said. "He really loves me. He can't help it, though he knows very well that the feeling isn't reciprocated. I fooled him for a year or so, but I couldn't keep it up. His meanness and his stupidity showed up every time he got drunk, and that was practically all the time. So after a while I couldn't help showing that I loathed him. Now he spends half his time thinking up ways to humiliate me. Funny sort of love isn't it?"

"IT'S VERY peculiar stuff," Omega interjected. "His love is no stronger than his natural ability to feel the emotion. The hypnosis merely keeps it constant. It doesn't improve it a bit. The same applies, in all likelihood, to the other hypnotically induced emotions.

"The citizens feel loyalty to Vargo only in proportion to each person's ability to be loyal. That's enough for him, of course. The same applies to devotion to employment.

"Some people are naturally more industrious than others. And even the most industrious can find occasional pleasure in other things besides work. So as a result the people of Detroit live fairly normal lives, outside of the phases which have been acted upon hypnotically by Vargo and his gang. And that keeps the majority so contented that it never occurs to them that their minds aren't entirely their own."

"It's wicked!" Nona exclaimed, fuming.

The aged man spread his hands eloquently. "It's all in the point of view. A queen ant would call it an ideal system. On the other hand, Mark thinks it's undemocratic."

"Mark will stop it," Nona said, confidently.

"No doubt," agreed Omega. "That's entirely up to him. But there's something else which interests me, at the moment. How would you like to stay in Detroit; make your home here? Disregarding, of course, the present type of government. Mark will change that, as you said."

Nona pondered a moment. "I don't know much about it," she confessed. "But what I've seen makes me think it's something like the cities I used to read about in the ancient books in Hartford... Even so, it's up to Mark. My home is where he is."

"There are amusements," Omega continued, ignoring the last. "Brilliant people, automobiles, libraries and everything you ever read about. Social life, and all sorts of entertainment. You should eat it up."

Nona's eyes lit up. She had read of twentieth-century life, and looked at it something like the way one would look at the enchanted existence in a fairy tale. But she said: "I'll leave it to Mark to decide. Why?" There wasn't any sense to telling Omega how she could set about making Mark think he wanted to do what she wanted him to.

"That's fine!" exclaimed the aged man, rising creakily. "I'll tell Mark you said you'd like it here. See you later. In the meantime look the town over more carefully. Gladys will show you around."

With an expansive and toothless grin which included both girls, Omega stepped through the door to the hall.

"No!" exclaimed Nona, leaping toward the door. "Let me tell him. Take me to him."

But the hall was empty.

CHAPTER XIII

MEET AN ANCESTOR

MARK LOOKED AT the assembled men with deep satisfaction. Thieves they might be, but here a thief didn't necessarily have to be anti-social. These were free men and in Detroit free men had no place. It was steal or starve.

When men are confronted with that particular alternative, the answer is usually a foregone conclusion. At least in the case of hardy men who have no fear of consequences. There was no moral issue at stake, for there was no other acceptable course at hand. It would have been far more degrading to have a hand in furthering Vargo's plans, once they had realized the true situation.

Ira broke the silence. "You're one of us now, I suppose," he said. The tone made it a statement, rather than a question. "You will accept orders from me, naturally. Any difference of opinion we decide by vote. There are seventy-four of us at present, but all questions are decided by this council of five here. Agreed?"

Ira waved a hand to include himself and four others of the six thieves in the room. Tolon was one of the five.

"We now number seventy-five," Mark said, removing his helmet and unscrewing the wings. "If you gentlemen will excuse me, I've some important business to attend to."

Mark placed the wings in his pouch and the helmet over his unruly thatch of hair.

"Wait, friend Mark," Ira demurred. "You are too distinctive to roam abroad with Vargo's agents looking for you. Removing those wings isn't enough." He turned to Tolon, "Summon Derek."

Mark looked at Ira with a certain admiration. The squat leader of the thieves had an agile brain. Mark had said nothing about the wings, but Ira had deduced his reason for removing them.

Derek appeared, a skinny, bloodless wisp of a man, struggling with a large wooden box with handles on each side. He thumped it on the floor beside the table, and looked expectantly at Ira.

With a wave of his hand, Ira indicated Mark. Derek stepped back a pace or two and examined Mark with a calculating eye. Then he frowned and walked around and looked at him from the rear. He made measuring motions with his hands and frowned some more. Mark was beginning to fidget at the lengthy examination. But finally Derek finished and opened his wooden box.

"You will please stand over here," he said.

Mark did as he was asked and cocked an inquiring eye toward Ira. The others grinned as Ira raised a finger to his lips.

"He's a scientist," Ira whispered, "but also an artist. So don't disturb his thoughts. He might make you look like a gorilla."

DEREK WENT to work with efficiency and speed. First he rigged up a peculiar lamp and turned it on Mark. It bathed him with a rose-colored glow. Then he produced a bottle and sprinkled a few drops of its contents on Mark's hair. He rubbed it in thoroughly and held the lamp on it for a minute. He followed that by moistening the eyebrows with the same liquid. The lamp momentarily bathed them also.

Derek stepped back and surveyed his work. "Perfect," he approved. "Now for the face."

A jar of some peculiar plastic material next made its appearance from the box. Derek applied this sparingly, a little on the cheekbones and some on the jaws. Then he stepped back again, nodding cheerfully and regarding Mark from all angles.

He followed that with a small dab in the region of the Adam's apple, and a few more on the ribs. The calves of the legs also received attention. Then he carried the lamp around and played it on Mark's back, not missing an inch of his anatomy. A few minutes of this and he returned the lamp and the other accouterments to the box.

"Perfect!" exclaimed Ira. "His own mother wouldn't know him."

Not, Mark reflected, after six thousand years anyway.

Derek smiled appreciatively and left the room, struggling with his box. Ira went to a cabinet, fumbled for a minute, and came out with a pair of black trunks and a white leather belt. There were no places on the belt for weapons of any kind.

"Put them on," he directed. "Then look in the mirror behind that door."

The trunks fitted perfectly. Mark opened the door which Ira had indicated. Then he gasped in consternation.

There was a full-length mirror on the back of the door, but it wasn't Mark who gazed back at him. The gentleman in the mirror was a dignified old fellow, light-skinned and snow-white of hair. He was tall and erect, of course, but the years had otherwise taken their toll. There were lines on the face, and the prominent cheekbones and jaw made hollows in places where Mark didn't have them.

The cheeks appeared sunken, and the eyes burned deeply in their sockets. A prominent Adam's apple made his neck look thinner. Furthermore the chest, which had formerly been covered with a smooth layer of muscle, now displayed prominent ribs. The calves were disfigured by varicose veins.

Mark got over his surprise and decided that at least he made a fine-looking old geezer. Something like judge Hardy, in fact.

"The man's an artist," said Ira. "A touch here and there and he's added forty years."

"That hair's more than a touch," said Mark. "The skin, too. The lamp did that, I suppose?"

"Derek's own invention," Ira said. "Its effect is the opposite of tanning. It bleaches the pigment. On the hair an acid aids the process. It'll grow back normal, however. And the skin will tan again. The plastic can be removed with chemicals.

"I'll give you a belt with weapons if you want, but it'll look out of place. A man of your age is exempt from army duty. You can tuck your automatic inside the belt. There's a thong in there to hold the barrel."

Mark left without weapons of any kind. He had tried putting the automatic under his belt, but found that it was uncomfortable when he moved. He didn't need one anyway.

IT WAS dark and there was no moon. He was glad of that, for his new shade of skin made him a lot more conspicuous than his former deep tan, and he had a bit of burglarizing to do. It would, however, effectively disguise him if he should run across anyone who had been furnished with an accurate description of him.

With only a quick glance to see that he was unobserved, Mark rose vertically in the air. High above the rooftops, he looked down upon the city, trying to orientate himself. The winding streets, when Tolon had led him to the den of thieves, had left him with a very confused idea of the actual direction of Vargo's palace.

After a minute he sighted it, away to the north. Not bothering to erect a shielding screen of moving air, he dashed directly toward the palace. Whipping fingers of wind combed through his white mane, and he felt a fierce exultation at its bite on his uncovered body.

The palace loomed larger as he sped toward it. A massive building, it was plainly visible at a height, though from the ground it would have been shielded almost entirely by the thick grove of trees which surrounded it. The lower floor was darkened, but its shape was clearly delineated by the rows of lighted windows of its upper stories.

Several of these winked out as Mark approached.

With a rush he halted his flight directly in the middle of a sheer granite wall which composed one side of the structure. He hovered momentarily at the edge of a lighted window, then left it to explore another. That one had showed him four uniformed guards, busy at a card game.

The next one he investigated even more briefly. It was a bedchamber, and two palace maids were preparing for a night's rest.

Several more windows brought similar results. Either he saw palace menials or guests. Some were reading and some were preparing for bed.

Once he saw two guards fencing, and apparently very earnest about it. Twice he looked in on feminine menials entertaining palace guards. All in all Mark was very annoyed with himself, when he finally retired to the roof to think the problem out.

Eavesdropping and Peeping-Tom routines were out of his line, and they tended to upset him. Also they caused slight color to diffuse his hollow cheeks. He wasn't looking for maids.

He wanted to find the Ancestors.

While Vargo was certain to have placed every protection about his own person, Mark didn't think he would take the same precautions with the Ancestors. And they were, therefore, the logical place to insert the entering wedge.

Mark gazed out over the city, trying to reason out a plan for locating these gentlemen. As he watched, the city was making ready for the night. Light after light was blinking out, as the occupants of the houses went to bed. But the busy streets were still ablaze, and probably would be for several hours.

Abruptly Mark leaped from the roof and descended the face of the granite wall. He was kicking himself for not having thought of the answer sooner.

None of the Ancestors was young. They would naturally have sought their beds some time ago. He hesitated a moment before perching on a darkened window sill. There were plenty of windows without lights, by now, and the odds were against picking the right one. There were five Ancestors. And there were thirty or more darkened windows. But there seemed no way to narrow down the odds. He had to take a chance. Probably several. The Ancestors' rooms would probably be good ones, not the simple bedchambers of the menials, but there was no way to tell which was which, when they were dark.

MARK WASTED no more time. Hinged windows swung inward after a moment of fumbling, and he cautiously lowered himself to the floor, just as cautiously he made his way across the floor, moving his sandaled feet slowly and feeling for any furniture which might be in his path.

His arms were outstretched before him, groping for the opposite wall. He had observed that most of the doors were directly opposite the windows on this floor, and that was what he was making for. He had also observed that light-switches were in the same handy positions beside the door-jamb as they had been in his own day. It was his plan to snap on the light and observe the identity of the person in the bed. Then, if it wasn't an Ancestor, he would be out the window in next to no time, probably without even awakening the sleeper.

Mark was not a mouse and he was slightly more than a man, but his plans did occasionally miss fire. This one did badly.

He had feared it, having noticed that all the bedchambers were not alike, or even furnished similarly, but he couldn't possibly have been prepared for what happened.

Each foot, as he stretched it forth, was an independent exploring agent, not even being required to bring itself to the floor to sustain his weight. For until it had reached forth for a distance equal to a full step, Mark kept his weight on the other one, ready to bring back the first if it should contact a piece of furniture.

But he couldn't know, when one of his feet progressed to the distance of a full step, and encountered nothing, that he had placed it beneath the edge of a bed which was directly in his path.

He realized his mistake when he placed his weight on the foot and brought himself forward. The side-board of the bed caught him on the shin. With a grunt, he toppled forward. Instantly a pair of arms wrapped themselves about him and held him.

Mark checked the chopping swing of a balled fist when he heard little delighted cooings, in the region of his left ear. A pair of soft lips found his own, and kissed him most thoroughly. Being a gentleman, Mark obligingly kissed back.

"Sugar," cooed the voice. "I never thought you'd get up the nerve!"

With a vagrant thought concerning the cowardice of a certain "Sugar," Mark placed the lady in a restful hypnotic trance, and left by way of the window. She would awaken in the morning with no memory of the fact that she had been rudely awakened. And disappointingly abandoned.

THE NEXT darkened room was on an upper floor, and as a result of his recent experience, Mark changed his tactics. As soon as he was inside, he slowly rose to the ceiling and groped toward the far wall. In some respects this was a more successful procedure, for there were no beds on the ceiling. There was, however, a chandelier. It jangled musically when he struck it.

"Wash at noise?" said a voice, both sleepy and alcoholic. "Who's hanging around?"

"Just a mild earthquake," Mark reassured him.

"Oh," said the voice, mollified. "Par' me."

A lusty snore sounded as Mark eased out of the window.

The next room should be the one, Mark mused. Three being a lucky number. Experimentally, he tried one on the extreme top floor. It had occurred to him that the Ancestors might seek the greatest distance from the sounds of the street. This time he reached the light switch without encountering either beds or chandeliers. He snapped it on—and didn't bother to turn it off. His guess was right.

One of the Ancestors lay on the bed, and a quick glance told him that no one shared the room, and that the door was securely closed.

The Ancestor was the youngest of the five, probably only in his early fifties. He awakened and shielded his eyes from the glare of the light. Mark was ready to prevent an outcry, but saw immediately that it wouldn't be necessary.

"Who are you, old man?" asked the Ancestor, conversationally. "And what do you want in here?

Mark grinned. "I'm the man who got Vargo so mad this afternoon."

The Ancestor peered at him in wonderment, recognizing him after a close scrutiny. "You've certainly aged since then," he said. "Have a seat. Tell me about yourself, and this power of flight. It's *telekinesis*, isn't it?"

Mark explained, as well as he could, the manipulation of nature's unlimited supply of penetrating energy waves.

"A sixth sense," diagnosed the Ancestor, "It is probably controlled by both sensory and motor nerves, partially automatic and partially voluntary, and entirely within the brain. Don't suppose you'd care to let me dissect?"

"Not just now, if you don't mind."

The Ancestor's eyes twinkled. "Unreasonable, I call it," he pronounced. "You came here for some reason. What is it?"

"I want to hear all about you Ancestors," Mark said. "How you regard Vargo, what your aims might be, and just why you cooperate in making slaves of two million people."

The Ancestor frowned. He did it thoroughly, as if from long practice. His eyebrows were bushy, incongruously so, and separated, precisely in the center, a delicate, aristocratic face and a high forehead surmounted by a thick thatch of iron-gray hair. His body was slight, Mark noticed, as the man swung his legs from the bed and began pacing the floor, blissfully oblivious to his ridiculous appearance in a short pink nightshirt.

CHAPTER XIV

DISCUSSION WITH A CONDOR

"I'D BETTER START at the beginning," he said. "You'll need the whole story, and even then you'll find it hard to believe.

"My name is Thomas, Jan Thomas. I was only twenty when the war broke out, but I'd already achieved some success in my line—bio-chemistry. The first draft hit me and I was put to work in a laboratory. New and deadlier micro-organisms were wanted. It was a rotten job, but we didn't ask questions in those days.

"Fortunately, it didn't last long. I never did get to the point of developing anything new. None of the millions who must have died in that war can blame me.

"A bomb hit the laboratory, very early in the war. I know it was early, for the war must have lasted years, and the bomb landed just two months after I was drafted. It was a gas-bomb, something new, and killed everybody in the place, including myself.

"I remember it hitting the roof and tearing a big hole in it. I was just thanking heaven that none of the wreckage had struck me, when I began to experience trouble in breathing. There was no odor, and I don't think there was any poison present. It just seemed that the air was becoming denuded of oxygen.

"I felt the same way once when the oxygen began to get low during a stratosphere flight. But I forget, you aren't familiar with such things."

"Go ahead," Mark said. "I understand you."

"I just wanted to bring out the fact that my body wasn't damaged in any way. I merely died of suffocation. Otherwise I might have stayed dead, which would have been a good thing. As it was, I woke up. That was about thirty years ago.

"Vargo'd reassembled the atoms of my body. If I had been killed in a manner which had ruined my body, the atoms would have been reassembled in their last setup and I would have died again—perhaps never even lived. So that explains how I got here.

"**THE REST,** why I cooperate with Vargo, is entirely out of my hands. At first it seemed the most natural thing in the world. He was a splendid fellow, with high ideals and a brilliant mind—a visionary of the most benevolent sort. He pictured a world lifted from barbarism and restored to its former high state of civilization.

"He talked of educating benighted peoples and fostering the spread of culture. He wanted to give to the entire world the fruits of his genius.

"As you may know, you can't start an argument with a true scientist by such methods. The scientist seldom plans anything else. He doesn't lust for power or wealth. He is interested only in learning new facts. While he may not have any great desire to advance mankind, he certainly has nothing against the idea. It seems all to the good.

"I worked, and so did the others, in the fine laboratories furnished by Vargo. We worked under his direction. He would suggest a line of endeavor and we'd follow it. Most of the work was merely duplicating from our memories, the things already known to twentieth-century science."

"How about Vargo?" asked Mark. "You changed your mind, eh?"

"Yes. Though several years went by before we did. I, for one, came to my senses when I realized that certain phases of my work were entirely alien to my nature. I had hated the idea of developing deadly germs, when I had been drafted in the war. Yet I realized that Vargo had talked me into thinking that it was all right to do so for him. He had broached the subject one day, about twenty years after he brought me to life.

"He said the advancement of civilization might be balked at by certain self-centered feudal lords. He suggested that our cause was worth fighting for. The others were developing weapons in case this became necessary. Machine guns and rifles were being made.

"It was only fit that I do my part and supply our army with cultures of germs to be placed in the water supply of any city which opposed us.

"I went to work, satisfied, and it took me a long time to realize that mine was a horrible task. Something I loathed. I told the others. We went to Vargo immediately and declared ourselves, refusing to have any more part in his plans. He hypnotized us more thoroughly than ever, and we went right back to work again! But from that moment on we knew what a rotten beast Vargo really is. He'd had the five of us hypnotized ever since he woke us, and we didn't even know it!"

"You're all opposed to him, and yet go on anyhow?"

"All of us," echoed Thomas, his eyes dropping wearily. "Try as we might, it is impossible to disobey his hypnotic commands. I'll go right back to work tomorrow preparing endless vials of deadly bacteria."

"No, you won't," said Mark.

Jan Thomas looked up, startled. His eyes met Mark's and froze. Their gaze was locked for a long minute, then Thomas relaxed.

"Your mind is free now," Mark told him. "I've erased all former hypnotic suggestion. Tomorrow you go to work for me. We'll smash Vargo and his little war!"

A LIGHT shone in Jan Thomas' eyes which hadn't been there before. He felt release from the slavery which had held him for so many years. Tomorrow he wouldn't fill little vials full of deadly cultures, and feel that every time he prepared one of them he was dooming hundreds of innocents to a loathsome disease-racked death. Tomorrow he would....

"What do you plan?" he asked. "Don't forget that Vargo has been working at this for more than a decade. And that he's resourceful, a genius."

"I'm not forgetting," Mark assured. "Where are the others?"

"In the next room is Carl Bach," Thomas said. "The others are on the floor beneath. I'll have to guide you to their rooms."

Mark nodded. "Stay here. I'll be back when I've taken care of Bach."

The fastening on the window of the next room was out of reach of Mark's fingers. The hinged panels were open a few inches but not quite enough for him to reach in and unfasten them. Mark went back into Thomas' room. He had just reached it when there was a shout from the hall.

Jan Thomas turned white. "That was Bach. He must have seen you and raised an alarm. They'll search all the rooms!"

"Then I'd better leave," Mark grinned. "I'll be back tomorrow, night and get the rest. You go about your work and pretend nothing's happened. But see that the cultures are dead when you put them in the vials. See you tomorrow."

Mark ascended straight up as soon as he was clear of the window. He attained a great height before he started out for the thieves' headquarters. He didn't speed as he had when he came to the palace. He floated along leisurely. A plan was stirring, fitting together in a way which promised to be workable. He was so busy putting the pieces together that he failed to notice that he wasn't alone in the air. Nor was he aware that he had company until a huge bird flew directly in front of him. His eyes followed the creature and saw it circle him, eyeing him warily.

"Scram," Mark muttered, and put on speed.

The bird seemed disinclined to take advice. It followed, beating the air powerfully.

Mark kept an eye on it, half expecting it would attack. Its beak, he observed, made a vicious weapon. Nor were its talons puny either. Mark wasn't really afraid, but he watched it closely. If it made any attempt to attack, he would put on a burst of speed which no bird could equal. Experimentally he put on a few more knots. The bird kept pace, even gaining a little.

Judging from its size, Mark decided it must be an albatross, though he didn't know much about ornithology; and it might be a roc or something.

Surprisingly, the bird kept up. It held that position for several seconds, still eyeing Mark as though trying to decide if he were edible.

"Do I know you?" the bird finally asked.

Mark slowed abruptly. The bird did likewise, only an arm's length distant. "What species are you?" Mark asked.

"Condor," snapped the bird. "Though I think it's rude to ask. I didn't inquire whether you were a gorilla or a chimpanzee."

"I don't know any condors," Mark claimed. "Go away."

"You'd look better with a beard," remarked the condor.

MARK WAS chagrined to note that indeed he *had* a beard—a long flowing white one, which whipped merrily in the breeze. "I don't want a beard!" he howled, and wrenched at it with both hands. This caused a surprising amount of pain, for the thing was real. It had actually grown there in the space of an instant.

"You ought to know better than that," said the condor. "When I make anything, it's real. And when I want to talk don't tell me to go away. It makes me mad."

"Okay, pal. Stick around and have a nice long chat. I was only fooling. How about removing this bush?"

The condor looked at the beard appraisingly. "I think you ought to keep it. It's very distinguished looking. Long and silky, like the tassels on a bathrobe. I'll bet you couldn't raise one as good in twenty years."

"Look, friend. I don't want a beard," Mark protested. "And if I did, I wouldn't want a beard that looked like the tassels on a bathrobe. So be nice, will you?"

"Don't bother me with trifles," the condor said shortly. "Shave it off yourself. I just dropped in to see how you liked Detroit."

"It'll be all right when I get it straightened out," Mark said, stroking the whiskers experimentally.

"You'd like to settle here, wouldn't you?"

Mark ceased his stroking. "I intend to settle here," he said. "This is going to be the center of a new America. I'm going to spend the rest of my life, if necessary, to make it happen. Civilization will spread out from here in waves, until all of America has reached the stage where it was when the wars broke out. But it will spread out naturally—not by force."

The condor abruptly ceased being a condor. It changed to the old man who had left Nona a few minutes before. "You don't say," said Omega. "Aren't you going to a lot of unnecessary trouble? I mean, isn't it enough to see that the peoples of the world don't keep warring on each other, and let them advance of their own accord?"

"Why is it?" countered Mark. "I've brought innovations which improved living conditions in Norway. Here in America even more can be done, because so much of the population is still living in the ruins of the old cities and has saved some of the former culture. Everything which Detroit now has, can be spread to other cities. Some day I'll have America back where it was in the twentieth century!"

"And that was no bargain." Omega fell silent for a minute. "Suit yourself," he finally said. "But my main interest here on the earth is to see that the new race thrives and develops. That's why I brought you here in the first place."

"I don't get it," said Mark. "I thought you wanted me to put the kibosh on this war."

"Only incidentally, my boy," said Omega. "I merely mentioned it because I knew you would start to work on it anyway. It really isn't important. A few thousand slaughtered humans won't affect the grand total very much. And if the humans don't care, why should I? I brought you here primarily to show you a place which I knew you'd like. A place at least as civilized as Norway."

MARK FROWNED. He could understand Omega's viewpoint concerning slaughtered humans, though he didn't subscribe to it. And it always jarred him when Omega expressed his contempt for humanity in general, though he could see the reason for that also.

"Why?" he asked.

"I told you, you dope. The new race has to multiply, and you have two kids, both of whom are now in Norway."

Mark frowned again. "I think I see what you're driving at," he said. "You want me to bring one of the kids here and leave the other in Norway?"

"Good boy," lauded Omega. "I even delved into your inhibitions and provided for them, though they're silly—very silly."

Omega beamed, very proud of himself, but that seemed to have no effect on Mark's frown.

"I've been dodging that issue for a long time," he confessed. "And I can't say that I'm nuts about your solution."

Omega's beam faded. "What's the matter with it?" he demanded. "I know that your conventions were decidedly against family marriages, but that has nothing to do with you. Those conventions were gradually imbedded into humans because of the disastrous things which so often happened. But they only happened because there were strains of mental and physical weakness present in the parents of the unfortunate off-spring. That doesn't apply to you. Intelligent people should control inhibitions which have no logical reason for existence. Cast them off!"

Mark knew enough of human history to know that popular ideas on the subject of in-breeding were decidedly inaccurate. He remembered the long line of Northern European royalty which had produced a preponderance of genius in its ranks. And few of the marriages had been further removed than first-cousin unions. No weakness had resulted until a certain union with an outside family in which weakness was present. From that time on, the inbreeding had produced disastrous results. Physically disastrous, for the weakness hadn't been mental. Genius had still cropped up, even in his own era, though faulty hearing, hemophilia and other physical disorders had run rampant.

Still further back in history were examples more in keeping with his own problems. The Macedonian Dynasty of Egypt was the most notable. Rulers, all through history, considered it necessary to marry only those in their own exalted station of life.

With the Ptolemies this had assumed an exaggerated form, in that they considered none sufficiently exalted to qualify. The result had been a series of family unions not duplicated in history. Nor had there ever been such a phalanx of outstanding people to be found in one family. Soldiers, statesmen, inventors, scholars, builders; all of them had been centuries ahead of their contemporaries.

Mark remembered that they had also been somewhat addicted to murder but that was really the order of the day, and they would probably have been considered weaklings to abstain.

ONE THING was apparent, as Mark remembered his laws of heredity. That was that in-breeding accentuates characteristics. If physical weakness is present in the parents, progeny are likely to be cripples. If mental weakness is there, idiocy will result. There lies the danger.

On the other hand if no weakness is present, no weakness can be transmitted. Strength, both mental and physical, is perpetuated; even intensified. Examples of both states were to be found abundantly in the pages of human history.

"Cast them off, eh?" Mark echoed. "Just like turning off a spigot. Only it's not so easy. They're *my* kids, you know."

"Rank sentimentality!" raved Omega. "Kids are kids, no matter whose they are. You'd admit the advisability of my plan if they were somebody else's kids. Bring one here, and leave one in Norway. When they grow up they'll have forgotten each other. They're young yet. Simple, eh?"

"Foolish," diagnosed Mark. "After you convince me, you'll have to convince Nona."

"Tell you what I'll do," offered Omega. "You make up your alleged mind, and when you come to my way of thinking, which you will, I'll take care of Nona."

Mark looked absently at the ground, thinking fast.

He knew that Omega had certain scruples against using his powers to influence the minds of those he liked. It was even against his principles to read another's mind, except where some strong reason presented itself. So far he had never, without permission, done anything of the sort to Mark.

On the other hand Omega was a very practical guy. And this business of founding a race, superior both mentally and physically, to normal humans, was a pet hobby of his. On the theory that the end, in this case, fully justified the means, he might scrap his scruples and take an unfair advantage. That he had the power to do so, Mark was well aware.

It would be a simple matter for him to make Mark believe that it was a noble thing for his son and daughter to marry. And Mark still nourished some inhibitions, reasonable or not.

"Suppose you give me time to think it over," he temporized. "There's no real hurry. These mental quirks are deep-seated, you know. It'll take a while to reconcile the logic of the thing with the phobias I've held all my life."

"I'll gladly give you a little help," offered Omega. "I can erase that inhibition in half a shake."

"No, no. Let me battle it out myself. I'd rather my mental processes operate of their own accord. It's an old democratic principle."

"I'm a Republican myself," claimed Omega. "But have it your own way. I'll see you later."

The aged body vanished to the accompaniment of a loud clap of thunder. Omega had a hankering for the dramatic, even if he was a Republican. Mark descended into the city, his mind chaotic.

CHAPTER XV

TRAP

"WHO IS HE?" asked Gladys, when Nona returned to the room after making sure that Omega had really left.

"A distant relative, on my great-grandfather's side," said Nona, biting her lip.

"You obey his orders?" asked Gladys.

Nona looked startled for an instant. "It's easier in the long run."

"Then I had better take you to see some of the city," Gladys decided. "That's what he said. It's still early, and we're not far from the avenue."

Nona regarded her quizzically. "I'm a married woman, you know."

"You don't look much like one in that outfit," said Gladys, thoughtfully selecting a dress from her meager supply, and handing it to Nona. It fit perfectly, though a bit blatantly.

Nona decided that Gladys would make a good guide after all, and took a hasty look in a mirror. A few deft touches and she was ready to go. Gladys had already repaired the damage caused by her husband's blow. She nodded approvingly when Nona turned from the mirror.

"You'll do," she said. "I wish I could take you to some of the places you'd really like. But they cost money, so we'll walk past them and pretend we don't want to be inside at all."

The walk was an adventure for Nona. Gladys led her past the gaudy fronts of several cabarets, reveling in the sounds of music and gaiety which floated through the open doorways. Nona noticed her fascination and wanted to know why she didn't stop in one of them.

"I told you they're expensive," Gladys said. "And besides ladies don't go in them alone. They must be escorted. It's the custom. If we went in without escorts, people would think we— Well, it wouldn't be nice."

Nona got the point. It surprised her mildly, for she hadn't quite made up her mind about Gladys. She had liked her from the moment she had seen her. Yet she wasn't at all certain what to expect from her. There was a streak of primness in her that certainly didn't go with her revealing dress or her painted face.

DEDUCTION CONCERNING the character of Gladys was abruptly interrupted when an automobile, resplendent with polished brass trimmings, pulled up in front of the cafe they were passing. A door burst open and a young man, dressed in faun-colored trunks and an impressive Sam Browne belt, almost fell out.

He recovered his balance, smirked foolishly, and went into a low bow which very nearly caused him to fall on his face. Nona and Gladys stopped, thinking the slightly inebriated young man had mistaken them for someone else.

Nona saw another young man preparing to alight, while the first was still trying to maintain his precarious equilibrium. This one seemed to be of a different stamp altogether. While the first was obviously under the influence of strong drink and seemed to be the spoiled child of a rich family, the second was cold sober, had a rollicking glint in his eye, and looked like a man of the outdoors. The corners of his eyes were faintly marked with crow's-foot wrinkles, and his skin wore a healthy tan.

He caught her eye and made a circular motion with one finger aimed at his forehead, then pointed it toward the other man.

The intoxicated man recovered from his bow with much effort, but still maintained his foolish grin. "You ladies will be my guests," he pronounced. "And I won't accept no for an

*Before Mark could prevent it, Jan Thomas reached up and
pulled a cord that was fastened to the head-board of the
bed—then struck feebly, but persistently, at Mark's face.*

answer." The last sounded a bit arrogant. He backed up the tone
by pointing at a little insignia in the middle of the cross piece of
his fine belt. Gladys gasped.

"One of Vargo's nobility," she whispered to Nona. "For heaven's sake—don't argue!"

The second man winked at both girls and took the other man's
arm, half supporting him. "This is Dene Baron," he said quietly.
"He wants to play a little trick on his family. We'll help him, eh?
It'll be lots of fun. My name's Tolon."

"Sure, sure," said Baron. "Lots of fun. There won't be any
after the war starts. And I'm going to show that family of mine
a few things."

"Nothing to be afraid of," assured Tolon, interpreting the
fright in Gladys' eyes. "He's harmless. He'd better be!"

Baron lost his foolish grin. For an instant he seemed almost sober. "You oughtn't to talk like that, Tolon," he complained. "I'm your friend. Didn't I give you everything in my pouch? Gold, too. Not silver."

"You didn't give it to me, brother," grinned Tolon. "I took it. First payment for my services. Come on, girls. Your first payment will be an outfit better than you ever hoped to own. Hop in."

Gladys put a hand to her mouth. "They think we're—"

"Come on," decided Nona. "We'll see what it's all about. You won't get hurt. This Tolon looks dependable."

TOLON FLASHED a smile and helped Gladys in. Nona followed and then Dene Baron. Tolon pulled down one of the folding seats and sat facing the others. To see them better, he turned on the dome light. His hand briefly caressed his automatic, as he turned his head to talk through the division glass to the chauffeur.

"Right over to Pretty Boy's little shop," he directed.

"You'll rue them words," said Dene, sleepily. "I oughtn't to pay you for tonight's work. You ought to be paying me. Imagine a common thief getting a chance to move in high society."

Tolon gave him a pitying look. "I'm a very common thief," he assured. "And whether your society's high or low is just a matter of point of view. I don't think you're so sure yourself."

Dene, who had allowed his eyelids to droop, suddenly snapped awake. "I'll find out," he said. "We'll see how they act, especially that family of mine. Now let's go and get a friend of yours for the other young lady."

"Nothing doing," said Tolon. "We'll get those clothes out of your dad's store, and we'll crash this party you've been talking about. We don't need anybody else."

"All right, all right," muttered Dene Baron, letting his eyelids droop once more. A soft snore followed.

"Would you mind explaining?" asked Nona. "Who is he, and who are you? What does he intend to do?"

Tolon grinned engagingly. "I told you who I am," he said. "Tolon, a thief. This scum came wobbling down a dark street a while ago, and I relieved him of a pouch full of gold. He wept on my shoulder and told me I was just the guy he needed.

"It seems that his family is forcing him into a marriage with the daughter of an influential family a step or two nearer to Vargo than they are. He wanted me to round up some of my friends and he'd pay us all... well, to go to a certain party that's in progress tonight. The idea is to queer himself with this other family, so they won't let him marry the girl."

"Then why us?" Gladys asked.

"I refused," said Tolon. "I told him I'd go alone, but I wouldn't call in any friends. You see I never saw this lad before. But he seems to be carrying the story through, all right. When I refused, he made another suggestion, that we get his car, which was parked on the avenue, and go pick up a couple of girls that—"

Tolon stopped suddenly, and flushed.

"Go on," prompted Nona.

Tolon rallied, manfully. "It doesn't matter exactly what he said. He's drunk, and besides he must have changed his mind, or else the liquor has affected his vision."

"Nice going," applauded Nona. Gladys' blush seemed destined to break all records.

"The car and chauffeur seem to back up his story," Tolon continued. "But even so I'm a bit leery of him. I suggested the new clothes idea. If he's really Baron, he'll have access to his dad's department store. We'll get a new outfit apiece. Then I'd advise you two to leave. It would be embarrassing to go through with it. I only agreed to picking you up so that I could suggest the clothes idea and check up on him."

BOTH GIRLS could guess what was next on the program. When they left, Tolon would take Baron to the party and stage a robbery. He could probably get away with it, once he gained admittance.

Gladys looked at Nona and shook her head. Nona smiled. "I

think we'd better leave now," she said, gently. "While our host is still asleep."

Tolon looked incredulous. "You mean you don't want new outfits? In the shape this boy is in, you could pick the best in the house."

Gladys shook her head again. "It would be stealing unless we went through with the bargain," she said. "And I don't think we'd better."

Tolon scratched his chin ruefully. "I forgot there were such ideas," he confessed. "It's up to you, however."

He turned to order the chauffeur to stop the car, then quickly whirled back again. But it was too late. He stared into the muzzle of his own gun! In the instant he had turned to speak through the division glass, Dene Baron had reached forward and disarmed him. He had acted so quickly that neither of the girls had been able to voice a warning.

"That wasn't really necessary, of course," said Baron easily. "I have another gun behind this seat. I just wanted to see if I could do it. You fellows aren't so clever after all, are you?"

He fished behind him and produced it, not letting the other one waver for an instant. Tolon was effectively covered now.

"What's the idea?" he asked. "Want your gold back?"

Baron chuckled. "That wasn't gold," he informed. "It was bait, and you struck at it. The inference is clear."

"I'm a fish, eh? Well I was a smart enough fish not to coax my friends to snap at your bait. And incidentally you might as well let these two girls out. They aren't thieves, you know. You heard them refuse to go to the store."

Baron shook his head. "No harm to take them along for investigation," he said. "After all they didn't say they were going to do anything to stop you, either. For all I know they may be shady characters."

"Don't be a fool," rasped Tolon. "You can see they're ladies. Why put them through embarrassment?"

Baron laughed harshly. "Who said any thing about a police

station? The police aren't worth much or you'd have been caught long ago. Vargo has picked the cleverest of the young nobles for this job. We use our own methods and hold our own court. And nobody carries word back of what happens. We'll have your bunch stamped out in no time at all. You see we know what you are!"

Tolon whitened visibly beneath his tan. "You've guessed why we are thieves. And you'd imprison two innocent people, rather than risk the others learning how I was captured?"

Baron smiled. "Precisely. But don't worry about the girls. They'll be entertained thoroughly. We'll turn them loose when we've caught the last of the seventy-four. I only picked them up as an excuse to get you to bring one of your friends to make a partner for the odd one."

"You know our number, too," observed Tolon.

Baron nodded. "We caught one about a week ago. He told us a few things, under pressure. Trouble was that he died too soon."

THERE WAS silence for the rest of the drive. Tolon didn't relax for an instant. But neither did Baron. He sat negligently holding one gun steadily in the direction of Tolon's stomach and the other at an angle which could be shifted to cover either of the girls in a split second.

He was wedged sideways in the corner of the broad back seat of the car and could easily watch both Tolon and the girls. He may have looked the part of a weak son of nobility, but he certainly handled his guns convincingly.

Nona wasn't sure whether to be frightened or not. For although she hadn't bargained for anything like this, it might lead her to Mark. And that was what she wanted most.

On the other hand she didn't like the idea of prison, and she had a lot less confidence in her own powers since she had noticed that guns were one of the commonplaces of this city. A deceptively powerful body and a knowledge of combat of all sorts were of little value against bullets.

She hadn't known that they existed until she had seen Baron

go into action. All but the butt had been hidden by Tolon's holster and she hadn't recognized the gun for what it was. But when the whole weapon came into view she knew instantly, for such things had been adequately described in the ancient books she had read in Hartford.

Gladys, a normal woman, was in no doubt about whether she should be frightened. Reason had nothing to do with it. An icy hand seemed to clutch at the pit of her stomach.

Nona felt her tremble and realized that she was next to panic. She admired the girl's pluck in not letting any evidence of it escape her lips. Surreptitiously she patted the arm which rested against hers. There was nothing else she could do, and it did seem to steady Gladys.

Tolon caught her eye and thanked her wordlessly. His eyes rested fleetingly on Gladys and then returned to Baron, apparently satisfied that the girl wouldn't do anything rash, and perhaps precipitate a slaughter.

Tolon was none too sure of the caliber of the man who faced him. He had guessed wrong once, and didn't intend to guess wrong again. And he suspected, in spite of the efficiency which Baron had already displayed, that it wouldn't take much to start him shooting wildly.

There was weakness in the man's face, and a certain indefinable look of cruelty. Tolon suspected that he would welcome the opportunity to use his guns. And most certainly he would use them if he thought his own skin was in danger.

Tolon remained quietly watchful, regretting most mightily the presence of the girls. Without them, he could have risked the noble's marksmanship. But with them in the car he was helpless.

The driver had apparently been given his instructions long before. He stopped the car in front of a stone building, not far from Vargo's palace, and opened the door of the tonneau. An automatic in his hand motioned the girls to get out.

A lone pedestrian took notice as the party entered the building. He scowled, but in the darkness neither of the men with the guns saw the expression.

They might have wondered if they had, for people seldom scowled in Detroit when anyone was ushered into a prison. People who went into a prison at the point of a gun were invariably ones who failed to obey the wise rulings of the great Vargo, and therefore, were getting their just deserts.

But neither Dene nor the chauffeur saw the scowl and the man went on his way, speedily and with purpose.

CHAPTER XVI

CHAPEAU BY VARGO

MARK'S MIND WAS far from placid when he sought out Ira, leader of the thieves. As if he hadn't had enough on his mind, Omega had given him a new worry. Cagily, he hadn't displayed too strong an opposition to Omega's plan, but he certainly didn't think much of it, just the same.

If there was any possible way of solving the problem without accepting Omega's solution, he intended to find it.

Ira seemed pleased when Mark requested that they find a room where they could talk in private. He took Mark to his bedroom, assuring him that they wouldn't be disturbed.

"Nobody'd ever think of looking for us here," Ira said, chuckling. "I sleep in the daytime, and very little then."

They sat at a small table, a bottle of excellent wine between them. A dim ceiling light on the other side of the room cast heavy shadows and illuminated only one side of their faces. Ira's wide, bony features made that half take on a look of sinister strength, quite at variance with his appearance under a more even light.

For while Ira's face depicted strength, there was nothing really sinister about it. His was a calm, assured strength, unruffled and unyielding. His lips were wide, capable of portraying expression; yet seldom revealing an emotion. Wideset gray eyes, imperturbably calm, twinkled as they looked into Mark's.

"That's a fine set of whiskers you have there," he observed. "Remarkable growth in so short a time."

"It's a gift," explained Mark. "I hope it doesn't spread to the ears."

They talked, and Mark's hazy plan began to take solid form as he learned more about the organization of the thieves. The fraternity which Ira headed was composed entirely of men who had gone through Vargo's Vocation Board with a knowledge of its methods. Every man possessed a natural resistance against hypnotic suggestion, and also sufficient mental alertness to have been able to deceive the Board into thinking that he had responded to treatment.

Furthermore each man had rebelled, becoming a thief rather than work at his assigned profession in accordance with Vargo's planned economy.

Most of them were fairly young men, only recently banded together, though there were some who had undergone the Vocation Board's training many years ago, and were in their late forties. These older men had formed the earliest nucleus of the fraternity.

There were few of them because in the beginning Vargo had done all of the hypnotic conditioning himself. Few had the resistance to withstand him. It was only in more recent years that he had trained assistants to soften the subjects before he gave them a final treatment.

This latter system had given those with some natural resistance against hypnosis a chance to realize what was coming and to resist even Vargo's great power. As a result, the ranks of the thieves' fraternity had begun to swell only in the last few years.

The brotherhood was held together, not only because of the need for mutual protection, but because of a certain esprit de corps which had risen between them, by reason of the fact that they formed a class radically different from other men of Detroit. Out of a population of more than two million, they were almost the only ones in the city who were really free.

This distinction, carrying with it the necessity for secrecy, bound them together as nothing else could. A thief could talk to another thief with a knowledge that the other's opinions and thoughts hadn't been molded and conditioned by the hated Vargo. And when arguments arose the participants became even closer to one another than they had been before.

For each knew that the other had expressed his own thoughts, and had a perfect right to them. Differences of opinion bound them closer instead of separating them. They were the recognized marks of free minds. Other citizens seldom expressed any thoughts which weren't the direct result of the hypnotic influence under which they moved.

"HAVE YOU made no attempt to nullify any of the works of Vargo?" Mark asked. "Haven't you tried to do something to stop this impending conquest?"

Ira spread his hands, helplessly. "We are few," he pointed out. "Two million minds are intent on this war. They can't be influenced. To try would make us stand out like a damaged thumb. We'd be in jail in no time at all."

"Sabotage?"

"A mosquito stinging an elephant. It wouldn't be noticed."

"The elephant's hide is thick," Mark agreed. "We'll have to poison him. We'll work on his vitals."

Ira looked interested. "Don't forget the minds of those two million," he cautioned. "You could destroy all their guns, and they'd still want to go out with knives and arrows."

Mark nodded. "But as long as they're preparing, we'll have no trouble from that angle. The war can be delayed. A final solution, of course, will have to provide for knocking the idea out of their minds. But until I can work that out, we'll have to take steps to delay the war. And there aren't many days to act."

Hours went by as Mark's plan was worked out between them in detail. Ira did most of the figuring, once the essentials were explained to him.

The plan was simple enough.

It was based on the sketchy nature of the army which was

shortly to go forth to conquer the world. Vargo's inexperience with things military had provided the weak spot.

Caravan guards were the mainstay of the army. They were to be its officers; the prime movers in Detroit's war of conquest. The choice was natural, of course, for these men were hard-bitten fighters, who knew the tricks and habits of the nomads. They also knew the character of the land over which their army would move, and the facilities for defense possessed by the various cities they had visited. They were admirably suited to the task of guiding the destinies of an army. What they lacked in strategy would be more than made up by guns and numbers.

BUT THEY presented a weak spot, nevertheless. They numbered less than two hundred. Remove them and the army became a body without a brain. Mark's plan was to remove them.

He and Ira worked out the idea to perfection. Quite a few members of the thieves' fraternity had, like Tolon, come from the ranks of the caravan guards. They knew where their favorite recreation spots were located. Kidnapping the guards, or at least a large percentage of them, would be easy.

There were houses owned by the thieves which could be used to confine those who were captured, but Mark intended to make their imprisonment of short duration. As fast as the thieves brought in their captives, Mark would erase the hypnotic suggestions of Vargo and replace them with ones of his own. The caravan guards would become members of his own band, whether they wanted to or not.

It wouldn't suffice merely to free them of Vargo's spell. There would be some among them who would still like the idea of a war. Fire would have to be fought with fire. And Mark no longer had any compunction about exercising his power.

There would still be some of the younger nobles who were capable and adventurous enough to take part in the leading of an army. Ira already knew of several such, and to try to capture them would be out of the question. But fortunately their number was small, nor were they sufficiently versed to take full command of an army, over the type of country which was to be traversed.

Without the caravan guards to lead the army, the war would be delayed. A lengthy period of reorganization would be necessary, and during that time Mark hoped to be able to formulate a plan which would erase the desire from the minds of Detroit's people.

As the night wore on, thief after thief stopped at headquarters to report, before proceeding to his separate home for a day's rest. Ira collared them, one by one, and issued instructions. There would be a meeting in the late afternoon, and after dark the thieves would begin their task of rounding up the caravan guards.

Those of the fraternity who had formerly been with the caravans spent most of the day in planning and preparation. Upon them fell the job of leading small parties to the various places where their quarry could be expected.

There were several favorite stamping grounds of the caravan guards, and most of them were admirably suited to the business of kidnapping. These men were like sailors in the respect that when they returned from hazardous journeys of long duration, most of their time was spent in having a glorious carouse. Few of them were married, for theirs was a bachelor's business. They lived hard and they played hard.

Even now, when few caravans were being sent out because of the impending war, the guards considered that moment poorly spent which found them completely sober when there was opportunity to be otherwise. Cabarets of the noisier sort were doing a rushing business.

Twice, even before darkness had arrived, caravan guards were brought into headquarters by old friends who were now members of the fraternity. Each time, the guard in question was hilariously drunk, and supposed that he was being guided to a place where liquor was plentiful and the girls agreeable. Mark worked on them immediately, and the fraternity increased by two. Vargo's army accordingly lost two hard-hitting and cagey officers.

Night came, and several more trickled in. Force was required only once. More than twenty were duly operated upon by Mark's counter-suggestion. Then there came a lull. Almost an hour went by with no new arrivals.

"I have a little business to attend to," Mark told Ira. "You can hold any others who come in until I return."

Ira, so pleased with the way their plan was working that he was actually grinning, promised to take care of things himself until Mark got back.

HIGH OVER the roof tops, Mark sped toward the palace. His "little business" involved the second portion of his plan. Jan Thomas had a part in it, as well as the rest of the Ancestors. With their help he could strike directly at Vargo, no matter how well he was protected and guarded. Vargo would never suspect that his own tools were being used against him.

Mark perched briefly on the window ledge of Thomas' room, then floated across the ceiling toward the light switch. Reaching it he paused for a second before turning it on. There was something wrong, he instinctively knew, yet he couldn't place it.

There was no sound, except for the gentle snores which sounded from the position which he knew the bed occupied. That was all right....

Or was it? Abruptly he knew it wasn't. His last words with Thomas had been that he would be back again tonight. Why then, wasn't Thomas awake and waiting for him?

Alert and ready to act instantaneously, Mark snapped the switch. But apparently there was nothing wrong. The room was unoccupied except for the sleeping Thomas. Mark looked at the sleeping man, then dashed to his side and shook him.

Jan Thomas opened his eyes, alarm in his expression. Alarm, but no recognition.

His face looked pinched because of a peculiar night-cap he was wearing. The thing fitted tightly over his skull and covered the back and both sides of his head. Gathered tightly around his neck, it terminated in a wide, elastic collar which fit snugly under the chin. It was this contrivance which had caused Mark to awaken the man so roughly.

Before Mark could act to prevent it, Jan Thomas reached up and pulled a cord which was fastened to the head-board of the bed. The raucous whine of a siren split the night with its terrifying wail. As the sound was augmented by that of running feet in the corridor outside, Thomas struck feebly, but persistently, at Mark's face. The sounds of approaching feet converged at the door of the room.

Without hesitation Mark snatched up Jan Thomas bodily and slung him over a shoulder. The futile thumps of Thomas' fists on his back didn't slow him in the least as he made for the window.

A second was lost in maneuvering his burden out of the window. In that second the door burst inward. Bullets smacked against the frame of the window, and several others whizzed past his head.

Mark felt a momentary burning sensation along the skin of a thigh as he cast himself outward, but paid it no heed. His greatest fear was that one of the bullets had found a resting place in the body of Jan Thomas.

For a breath-taking hundred feet Mark and Thomas dropped toward the ground. Then, with scarcely twenty feet to spare, they swooped out of the fall and sped through the grove of trees, gaining altitude as they went.

Thomas kept up his incessant hammering, which made it pretty clear that he hadn't been hit by any of the flying bullets. The scratch on his own thigh, Mark knew, was already healed. But Thomas didn't have any of the remarkable blood which healed wounds almost as soon as they happened.

High above the city, Mark halted his mad flight. He twisted Thomas around in front of him and gave him the full blast of his hypnosis wave. Thomas only reached out with an intended haymaker and landed on his nose.

Abruptly Mark realized what was wrong. The night-cap was a shield! Holding Thomas with one hand, he ripped it off. The futile pummeling ceased immediately.

Jan Thomas was seized with a fit of trembling as he looked down at the city.

"Imagine you're in an airplane," suggested Mark. "Papa won't let you down… What happened?"

CHAPTER XVII

PLAN FOR PULLING TEETH

THOMAS FORCED HIMSELF to look up. "Vargo must have guessed. As soon as the search for you ended—zingo! He shoved all five of us into a hypnotic trance. I was the last and he must have discovered that you had released me from his influence. I don't know anything after that. Only that when I woke up it seemed urgent that I pull that cord."

But Mark knew how to get the information he sought. It was locked in Thomas' subconscious, whether he knew it or not. And Mark found it quickly.

When Bach had told Vargo that someone had tried to gain entrance at his window, Vargo knew that the only man who could have been there was Mark. He guessed why, and investigated to find if Mark had already reached any of his Ancestors.

Thomas, unwittingly, had told him. Vargo had then placed Thomas in a state of hypnotic sleep and left him in his bed to provide a trap when Mark returned. He had impressed only one suggestion; that Thomas pull the cord if anyone attempted to arouse him. Of the helmet, Thomas knew nothing.

Mark guessed that the thing had been devised by one of the other Ancestors, at Vargo's direction. Work had probably been started on it the instant that Vargo was aware that there existed a greater hypnotic power than his own. And Mark had shown him that, the previous afternoon.

By now there were probably several of the gadgets, inasmuch as Vargo was warned that Mark intended to strike at him through the Ancestors. It was conceivable that he would have all the palace attendants equipped with them.

Mark examined the thing and found it to consist of an extremely fine wire mesh, woven as a lining to the cloth exterior of the helmet. At a glance he couldn't tell what metal had been used, but guessed that it was lead. Whatever it was, it had effectually screened his hypnosis wave.

Once more his plans went a-glimmering. His greatest weapon was nullified by the existence of the screen. Morosely he carried Jan Thomas to the thieves' headquarters.

Several more caravan guards had been brought in during his absence. He treated them without enthusiasm. There was now a total of forty-two of the emancipated guards, and more were coming in. Before long Vargo's army would be practically bereft of officers.

But the measure was at best temporary.

The war would be delayed, but not called off.

Nor would the postponement be of great duration, either. Vargo was resourceful and it wouldn't take him long to realize that there was another class of men who were conversant with the ways of the nomads and thoroughly familiar with the layouts of the various cities on the conquest list.

Caravan guards weren't the only ones who had traveled to the lands which must be conquered. Every caravan carried a host of porters, laborers and ox-drivers. On occasion many of these were fighters as well.

And even those who had never been called upon to bear weapons in protection of their caravans had observed the methods of the regular guards. They were also familiar with the characteristics of the trails, and would know how to avoid ambushes. And they were familiar with the defenses of other cities.

It would be only a matter of days before they would be pressed into service, and trained for the job of directing the army.

THE NIGHT wore on, and in the intervals between the treating of new arrivals, Mark studied the problem of working out a complete plan for the frustration of Vargo's dream of conquest. He wracked his brain thoroughly.

And having had no little practice in wracking, he eventually devised a plan. At first glance, the difficulties attending its accomplishment made it appear useless and impractical. But he went on with it just the same.

The afternoon before, he had kicked himself for passing up the opportunity to operate hypnotically on Vargo himself. Well, it was still an idea, and he worked it in. Of course, *that* was one of the things which made his plan slightly on the impractical side, especially now that Vargo had a screen against hypnotism.

Mark remembered that he had conceived the thought after it was too late to put it into practice. The recollection had brought to mind the fact that such a course of action wouldn't be so simple as it had first appeared.

From a purely academic standpoint he considered its difficulties. In the first place, Vargo had accomplished his subjugation of the citizens of Detroit over a period of thirty years. It would take almost as long to unhypnotize the same people.

And he doubted that Vargo would live that long, even if he were able to make Vargo suddenly want to undo his life's work.

In the second place, some of the hypnotic suggestions which Vargo had impressed would cause disaster if erased. You couldn't dehypnotize a man who had been happily engaged in a certain occupation for a number of years and let him realize that he had no consuming passion for that kind of work.

Cases like that would have to be handled carefully. For those who got their only fun out of manufacturing war materials, a substitute suggestion would have to be made such as the delightfulness of making bridges or whipping up batches of insect spray. Otherwise a host of people would be left ambitionless and without any driving urge to live.

These things would take some time, of course, but Mark did solve the problem of removing the insane desire for a war of conquest.

And what a problem! Hypnotic suggestion was impressed on a timid mind by verbally repeating the desired suggestion. So-o—it was going to take plenty of time even to begin to undo the things that Vargo had accomplished over such an extended period. Verbal counter-suggestions would have to be given individually to each person who had been hypnotized.

Nice and easy, like pulling one tooth after another.

That, Mark knew, was what he would have to do if he tackled the job himself. And, reflecting dourly on such a state of affairs, he had an idea. It was, he told himself, a pushover. But perfect!

The thing was tailor-made. When Tolon went before the Vocation Board, Vargo had dwelt upon the suggestion that Tolon must believe that he was a wise and benign ruler and was therefore to be obeyed without question henceforth and forevermore. The clue was right there:

Almost the entire population of Detroit would react immediately and obediently to the *voice* of Vargo!

Mark remembered how much had been accomplished in his own day by certain European dictators, who used the hysterical qualities of their voices without even possessing the gift of hypnotic power. *Radio!* A science in which Mark was an expert and with which he could force Vargo to tell his people that war was no longer to be desired.

All he had to do was re-invent it.

COMPLETELY IGNORING the fact that he must first hypnotize Vargo and make him really the selfless individual he preferred to be, Mark asked Ira to call in some electrical experts.

"At this time of night?" Ira exclaimed.

Mark nodded. "Rout them out of bed," he ordered. "Pick men who have authority in the plants where they are employed. And be ready to sign a lot of checks. I'm liable to bankrupt the fraternity before the night's over. But I'll make you rich as a result. Detroit is going to have a new industry."

Mark didn't wait for the experts to arrive. He called for paper and drawing pencils, and went to work. Under his practiced hand plans began to take shape. He filled sheet after sheet of paper with detailed instructions on the construction of various items which go into the manufacture of a radio broadcasting station and a receiving set.

His memory went back six thousand years for the desired information, but in a matter of a few hours he was finished.

Long before the task was completed, the experts arrived and were immediately placed in an hypnotic trance. Mark trained their minds in this state far more easily than he could have done if they were conscious. Each fact that he taught them would be immediately available when it was needed.

Also was impressed the desire for secrecy in the manufacture and fabrication of the finished product. Co-workers of the various experts must be made to believe that the strange articles which each expert would develop in his laboratory were designed for different purposes altogether. Each man left with his plans and plenty of money to cover expenses, fully educated for his task.

Work was to be started immediately. A broadcasting outfit of moderate power would be in operation in less than two weeks. A hundred receivers would be ready for installation in halls and meeting places. The people of Detroit would soon hear from Vargo himself that war was no longer desirable, that there were other methods of lifting the rest of the world to Detroit's cultural status.

That heroic task completed, Mark all of a sudden felt considerably deflated. He had started the ball a-rolling; a ball which promised to bounce off the stone wall of Vargo's impregnability. And there was no sense in trying to plan a way past the man's defenses. Any plan he might devise had too many jokers in it.

There were too many ways in which Vargo might circumvent anything he might think up. Attack by way of The Ancestors was out. Similarly it might be useless to show himself at the palace. He already had sufficient proof that Vargo had ordered him shot on sight....

Mark suddenly remembered that he didn't look quite the same as the fellow who had first aroused the dictator's ire. Vargo had ordered a bronzed young man with a winged helmet shot on sight. Then he had shown up at the palace as an old man. Vargo had forced that from the mind of Jan Thomas. And he had ordered the old man shot.

Suppose he assumed a new disguise?

Mark growled suddenly, remembering the helmets. Then abruptly he cast the whole subject from his mind, realizing that when the time came he would have to meet a set of conditions which couldn't be planned for now. He would probably have to organize a battalion from the membership of the thieves' fraternity, and take the palace by storm. His mind, momentarily unoccupied, reverted to more personal problems.

Omega—that blasted, meddling, lovable old remnant of a disfranchised spider....

CHAPTER XVIII

LET'S GO TO PRISON

HIS EYE FELL upon the slight form of the one Ancestor he had managed to free. Jan Thomas, refreshed from an entire day and night of sleep, was busily chatting with a pair of the older thieves. In them, it seemed, he had found kindred souls.

Both had been technicians, before they had joined the fraternity, and still were intensely interested in scientific research. One of them was a chemist; the other a biologist who had once had a hand in the growth ray's early development. The latter was responsible for the perfection of the nutrition solutions which were constantly fed to the abnormally fast-maturing vegetation.

Mark walked over to the three and listened for a few minutes. They were talking over plans whereby they would collaborate on some obscure research in which all three were interested, it gave Mark an idea.

"Wait a minute," he interrupted. "I've got a job for you. Especially you, Thomas. Get a syringe. I want to give you a sample of my blood to work on."

Ira, Jan Thomas and the two old men gasped in unison as the glass tube of the syringe slowly filled itself with his blood.

"Duplicate that," said Mark. "Find a liquid which, when injected into the veins of a healthy animal, will cause its blood to become like mine. Experiment on animals only, and let me know the instant you achieve success. Don't use it on a human being. I must first test the animal which you have changed."

To be certain that his orders would be obeyed. Mark once

more used his power. Jan Thomas and the two old men would be unable to do other than obey. Ira watched and listened as he repeated the order. He was impressed by the repetition, but didn't realize that the three were under Mark's hypnotic wave. Even as Mark released them, Ira was none the wiser.

"What is its particular value?" he asked—"other than the value of ordinary red blood?"

For answer Mark took a dagger and sliced deeply into the flesh of his arm. A smear of blue blood appeared—and then the wound healed, leaving no trace. Ira's eyes betrayed his astonishment.

"If they succeed," Mark said, "certain worthy ones will be injected. It has other valuable properties as well."

Mark sat down at a table and dismissed the entire contents of the room from his consciousness. He wanted to think; to think more deeply than he had done for some time. Ira, several of the new converts, and a half dozen of the older members of the fraternity were present, but he cast them completely out of his mind.

He had made an initial step in a course of procedure which would have never occurred to him under other circumstances. Inwardly, the thought of his own temerity made him cringe with apprehension.

OMEGA HAD been his guiding angel since the moment of his awakening, and it wasn't easy suddenly to take a course completely at variance with the omniscient being's wish. He was knowingly running counter to the desire of one who could destroy him in an instant. Destroy the whole earth, for that matter.

It was like flying in the face of a god more mighty than Jupiter. Except that instead of a legendary deity, of doubtful potency, and only rumored authenticity, Mark was contemplating the defiance of a very real entity, one of proven and adequately demonstrated power.

Mark thought. He thought, because it wasn't too late to back out of his decision. He could easily stop the three scientists from analyzing the sample of his blood. He could erase the memory of it from their minds, and Ira's as well. And as he thought, he became more apprehensive as to the reaction of the unpredictable Omega.

Omega liked him. But he liked Mark because he thought Mark was considerably different from the average, emotion-ridden human. He had revived him because Mark was a man of logic, as well as a man of good character. Omega had always insisted that emotion was all right in its place, but that its place was subordinate to cold, rational logic. Where the two conflicted there was no room for compromise.

Mark knew that he was right, and yet he was human enough to refuse to apply the rule in his own case. And there, he greatly feared, was a point where Omega might forget that he liked Mark.

Mark might be placing himself, in Omega's mind, as just another human: worthy of sublime contempt, and to be treated accordingly.

And "accordingly" might take on some obnoxious forms. For Omega had a peculiar sense of humor, as Mark well knew. When he found that his pet plan for populating the earth with the superior descendants of Mark and Nona had been tampered with—indeed, wrecked completely—it was hard to say what he might not do.

Mark might find himself transformed permanently and irrevocably into a loathsome reptile. Most anything could happen, and probably would.

Mark suddenly jumped to his feet and laughed. Let Omega fry! He liked the old duffer and valued his friendship. But Mark was a man, and a man had to stand on his own feet, come what may. He'd go through with it.

If the scientists succeeded in duplicating his blood, he'd inject it into quite a few people before he turned up his toes. He'd be careful and pick out only those he knew had few vicious instincts, and then hope for the best.

And unless he was very much wrong, it would come out all right.

AT THAT moment the outer door opened and another caravan guard was brought in, this one feet first. He was either very intoxicated or one of the boys had massaged his scalp with a club.

"What's the score?" he asked Ira.

"One hundred and four," was the pleased answer.

"Any casualties on our side?"

Ira hesitated. "No," he answered. "Not tonight. Though a couple were bunged up a bit. Last night, however, Tolon was captured."

"Tolon!" Mark exclaimed. "Why didn't you tell me?"

"I didn't know it until just now," Ira said. "While you were sitting there, one of our men came in, pretty much the worse for wear. He'd gotten in a fight last night and spent the day recovering his senses. He just remembered that before he got in the fight, he saw Tolon taken into the private prison of the nobles."

"Where is he?"

Ira led Mark to one of the bedrooms. He saw the pain-wracked body of a wizened, middle-aged man writhing on the bed. His eyes were wild with the delusions of fever and weakness.

"He's injured badly," Ira said. "I've sent for a doctor, one of our own men."

Mark bent over the man and looked in his eyes. Immediately he became still, and the pained look left his face. Across his forehead was a jagged cut, its edges inflamed and swollen.

Mark passed a hand over the cut and held it there for a few seconds. The inflamed condition indicated that infection had set in, and Mark knew that his hand would kill the germs which caused it. Omega had once told him that the radioactivity of his blood sent emanations for several inches outside his body, and were sure death to any micro-organism they touched.

He had used this quality many times in the past dozen years to heal the untended wounds of the hardy Vikings, who were inclined to ignore any injury which left them with all limbs intact.

The man's eyes opened and the light of sanity returned to them.

"Take it easy, fellow," said Mark, soothingly. "Tell me what you saw last night, if you feel strong enough."

The man cleared his throat and began. His voice was weak and rasping at first, but gained strength as he went on.

"The nobles' prison," he said. "Where they take the ones who work against Vargo—the ones who aren't hypnotized. Dene Baron and another man had them covered with guns. I waited down the street but they didn't come out while I was there."

"They?" asked Mark. "Was someone besides Tolon captured?"

"Two women. Girls, rather. Both beautiful. The nobles will keep them, but you'd better send after Tolon. He's the third to go in there in the last week and the others didn't come out."

Mark turned to Ira, who looked decidedly grave. "What is this nobles' prison?" he asked.

"We can't touch it," said Ira. "We've, never been able to get a man out of it. The nobles use it for special captives who rebel against the dictates of Vargo. Ordinary offenses are dealt with in the regular police courts, but the ones who go to the nobles' prison are never heard from again. They get no trial at all."

"Where is it?"

"Not far from the palace," Ira replied. "They say there's a passage between the two. The belief is that Vargo himself imposes sentence on any captives who are taken there. Poor Tolon. He was one of our best men. Always cheerful, and a demon in a fight."

Mark scratched his chin. "I don't like the way you used the past tense," he said. "I'd rather use the present when referring to Tolon. Take me to this prison, while it's still dark."

CHAPTER XIX

BLACKOUT FOR AN OLDSTER

A THIN CRESCENT of a moon was just setting in the west. In the east there was a faint lightening of the sky which would spread and increase in brightness as the seconds advanced. Mark knew that his time was limited when he sent his guide back to headquarters and soared toward the upper windows of the prison.

Accordingly he paid little attention to the noise he made as he wrenched at the bars of a window high up on the sheer face of the prison's western wall. Dimly, he could see a long gloomy corridor, only faintly visible by the glow which entered a similar window at its other end.

That window looked out toward the east, and the heightening of the light made him increase his efforts with the stubborn bars.

Finally, with a savage burst which almost pulled the skin from his hands, he wrenched them from their sockets, tearing loose handfuls of powdered concrete in the process.

He lowered himself into the corridor, dropping the last few feet to the stone floor. His sandals made a swift patter as he sped along looking for a staircase to the lower floors. There were cells in this corridor, but none was occupied. He guessed that this was an unused floor, probably out of service since Vargo's rise. It looked like an ancient place, probably once well populated.

But if, as Ira had said, it was only used for rebels against the authority of Vargo, there wouldn't be many occupants in the palace. There couldn't be many rebels, for one doesn't rebel when under the influence of hypnotism.

The lower floor of the building was windowless, Mark had noted, and it was there that he would find Tolon.

There was a stair entrance in the middle of the corridor. Mark passed it once without seeing it, for its door was the same as the ones which led into the cells. Fortunately it wasn't locked, and he saved the minutes he would have had to use in forcing it. It creaked protestingly as he swung it aside. He swore silently and hoped the sound couldn't be heard below.

THE STAIRWAY wound down in short flights, a barred door at each landing. Mark's quiet profanity attained new heights as each of the doors made known its objection to being moved. The noise couldn't be helped, however, and seconds were precious.

He moved down the last flight and was relieved to see a stone door at the bottom. A crack of light shone on the floor beneath it. If the sounds had been heard, he reasoned, someone would be opening that door to investigate. The fact that it was shut was a good sign.

Gropingly he fumbled for a knob or latch. The chances were against the door's being unlocked, but he hoped for the best. He hadn't thought to provide himself with a gun or anything which could be used as a tool to batter away a lock.

But as he groped he remembered the bars he had left on the floor beneath the forced window. One of them would make a good crowbar. On the other hand, it would make a lot of noise as well.

If the thing was locked, he might as well knock and demand entrance, trusting to luck and hypnotism from that point on.

His hand found the latch. The door was unlocked.

Cautiously he opened it, an inch at a time. This door was apparently resigned to being moved, for it made no protest. The crack at the bottom became wider, as he pulled the door toward him. Electricity made that light, which meant that there were guards in the room beyond. An electric light wouldn't be left burning for the prisoners.

Mark peered through the crack he had made. A blank wall met his gaze. A little further... The edge of a cell door came into view. The light came from a point to the left out of his line of vision. That's where the guards would be. A light cough from that direction confirmed his guess.

A little more... He could now see almost half of the cell door. Tolon might be back of that door! As soon as the stone portal moved enough for him to get through and see the guard, or guards, he would step forth without warning and hypnotize them on the spot. They mustn't get a chance to draw their pistols.

Suddenly the stone door let out a shriek of outraged, rusty hinges. As if the sound had touched off a spring, Mark leaped into the room, turning to face the direction from which the cough had come.

But he didn't complete the maneuver. His eyes passed fleetingly across the door of the cell he had been seeing, and then stopped abruptly, shocked by the sight they saw! In the cell was a vision of loveliness....

"Nona!" gasped Mark—and pitched to the floor.

HIS EYES had never reached the guard who had stood motionless, gun in hand, watching the slowly moving stone door. His ears hadn't been quick enough to catch the sound of the shot, nor the whine of the bullet that struck him down.

Nona bit at her knuckles as she watched the guard turn Mark over with a foot. For a second she thought....

But no, it was an old man who lay there on the floor. His skin was white, and less than five days ago she had seen the deep tan of her husband.

She had been sleeping on the cot against the wall when the shot had rung out. She must have dreamed that she had heard Mark's voice, the instant before the shot had awakened her.

Mark's hair was an unruly chestnut, and he was clean shaven. This poor old fellow was snow white and had a beard that must

have taken years of loving care to nurture to its present magnificent proportions.

She calmed herself when she became thoroughly convinced
that the man on the floor wasn't Mark Then abruptly she was
furious as the guard callously dragged the inert body across the
floor and dumped it in an unoccupied cell.

"Aren't you going to help him?" she yelled. "Call a doctor!"

The guard looked at her quizzically, then carefully spat on the
floor. "Take it easy, lady," he admonished. "He's dead. And if he
ain't he'd better be. People don't go busting into Vargo's jails and
then live to brag about it."

"A fine thing!" said Nona tartly. "How do you know he wasn't
lost? The least you can do is report it; Vargo will tear your ears
off if you don't."

The guard laughed. "Lost!" he scoffed. "How could he get in
here, if he was just lost… Say! How did he get in here anyway?
There's nothing back of that door but—"

The guard exploded into sudden activity. He peered into the
cell where he had placed the old man, then slammed the cell
door, locking it. Then he glanced up and down the cell corridor,
as if to make certain that everything was all right. Next he disappeared through the stone door which led upstairs.

A clamor came from the other end of the corridor. Gladys
wanted to know what had happened. Tolon was also curious. A
thief by the name of Forney added a feeble voice to the demands
for information. Nona obliged.

Forney had been in the prison for several days and his voice
was weak because he hadn't been fed. When he became weak
enough, Vargo would work on him. A similar fate awaited Tolon.
Vargo had failed to get any information from him by hypnotism,
for he had been fully prepared to resist and had resisted.

Torture was next on the program, though it had always failed
in the past, and would fail again. The members of the fraternity
were tough people.

ALTHOUGH FORNEY had little to console him in his imprisonment, Tolon was finding a certain enjoyment in the state. His cell was directly across from that of Gladys, and Gladys wasn't hard to look at.

He liked the shy way she looked across at him, especially when he caught her at it. The faint blush which had several times appeared in her cheeks when she glanced his way and found him intently admiring her, delighted him.

Nor was he greatly concerned or worried about coming events. He had been in quite a few tight places in his career, and had always come out with a whole skin. There was a certain ever-present buoyancy about Tolon's nature which made it impossible for him to conceive of disaster before it actually struck him.

It was more than likely, he figured, that when they took him out of the cell to torture him he would get a chance to turn the tables and escape, taking the others with him.

Sound of the guard's footsteps diminished in the distance as he trotted to the upper floors. But with their cessation, the prisoners became aware that other footsteps were nearing. They made a hollow sound, as if echoing against the walls of a narrow corridor. They paused and there came the sound of a massive iron lock clinking over its tumblers. A faint rasping of unoiled hinges followed.

A new figure appeared in the cell corridor, it was Dene Baron. Nona raised a clamor without delay, shaking the iron door of her cell.

"Quiet!" snapped Baron.

"I won't!" returned Nona. "See what you can do for that old man in the next cell. The guard shot him. *Do* something!"

Baron looked surprised, but went to look in the next cell. The white-haired figure lay limply on the floor. There was a streak of blue, dried and matted, in the center of the scalp. Baron reached for the ring of keys hanging on the opposite wall of the corridor, and fumbled with the lock.

"Where's the guard?" he asked.

"He went upstairs to see how the old man got in," Nona told him.

Baron hesitated, before opening the cell door, and looked extremely thoughtful. The three lower floors were windowless, he knew. A ladder was out of the question. The lowest windows were entirely too high for that. No buildings adjoined the prison, and therefore no access could be had from other roofs. The only outside door to the prison was impregnable. And the passage to the palace was securely locked. That left—nothing!

Dene Baron looked carefully at the supine figure on the cell floor. There was no discernible breath. Strands of the white whiskers had fallen across the lips, and they were motionless. The man was dead. There wasn't a doubt of that. But—was this the same man?

Dene Baron was no fool, and in any case two and two invariably added to four. Only a bird could have gained entrance to the prison through the upper floors. And while the man may have been here for some time, and had hidden on the upper floors, he still couldn't have come in through the front door or the passageway.

That left the windows, through which a bird might have flown. Or a man who could fly like a bird!

Baron had never seen such a man, but he had heard of one. A young man, bronzed, and wearing a winged helmet. Like a picture he had once seen of an ancient god called Mercury. But such a man could be disguised. He must find out.

STILL KEEPING a wary eye on the corpse, he unlocked the door. For while Baron was no fool, he did have a streak of superstition in his make-up. Millions of people had once worshiped gods of various sorts. There might be something to it. The story he had heard of the man who flew, certainly sounded like it.

And if he could fly, maybe he could do other things. Possibly he didn't breathe air like men. What nonsense! The guard had shot him and brought him down. A god wouldn't be brought down by a bullet. Gods were immortal.

With renewed confidence Baron strode to the side of the old man. He leaned over, looking for a wound, and also for signs of a disguise. Suddenly he tried to jump back, but was too late by a wide margin.

Fingers of tempered steel found his throat and throttled him. Eyes, burning with a wild intensity, bored into his. Frantically he pounded at the body of the old man, but felt himself getting weaker, moment by moment. Eventually he went limp and the fingers let him drop, lifeless, to the floor.

"Is he alive?" called Nona.

She was startled to see the aged man emerge into the corridor, staggering slightly and shaking his head with an expression of bewilderment on his fine old face. Dene Baron didn't reappear. The old man peered at her uncertainly and shook his head again.

He walked, touching the sides of the corridor to keep his balance, toward the other cells. Then he seemed surprised to find a few of them occupied. He looked at Tolon and Gladys, then finally at Forney, but made no attempt to release them.

Tolon watched the old man, a puzzled expression on his face. The aged figure was faintly familiar, but he couldn't quite place it. Long, white beard, hollow cheeks… He finally gave it up, deciding that the old fellow must resemble someone he had seen.

"Say, old man," he called. "Suppose you get that bunch of keys and unlock these doors."

The old man turned back at the sound of the voice, and crouched warily, but made no sign that he had understood. Finally deciding that no harm could come from the man behind the iron door, he relaxed and came erect. Then he crouched again, at the sound of footsteps coming from the direction of the stone door. When he identified the source, he quietly placed himself beside the doorway and waited.

He seemed to have regained more control of his legs, for he had walked to his position of ambush with a degree of certainty, no longer requiring a steadying hand on the wall.

The footsteps came nearer and the old man tensed. The guard

stepped forth from the doorway, and again the steel fingers sank into a soft throat. This time they didn't choke, slowly and thoroughly, as they had with Baron. The thumbs dug into the back of the neck and the fingers raised, forcing the chin up. It was a sudden twisting motion, and the guard's feet raised off the floor for an instant. Then the neck snapped, and the body became limp.

The old man held the body for a minute, the toes barely touching the stone floor. Then he cast it down, his eyes again burning wildly. Like a trapped animal he looked up and down the corridor, then strode swiftly toward one end of it.

The heavy door to the street seemed to baffle him, though its latch was a simple one. He turned back and stopped at Nona's cell. Wondering vaguely why she shrank back at his approach, he marveled at her lithe body.

HE SUDDENLY decided that he wanted this beautiful creature. He didn't know why—he just wanted her. He frowned at the bars of the door which separated them. Grasping them, he shook. They rattled with a loud clatter. The sound scared him and he stepped back, snarling. But when the door showed no sign of attacking him, he gingerly approached it again.

Suddenly taking a bar in each hand, he pulled, exerting every ounce of strength. Gratifyingly, the door bent in the middle, sliding the tongue of its lock out of the socket. He pulled it open and stepped inside.

Nona shrank back into the depths of the cell. The old man walked after her smiling in anticipation. He reached forth, grabbed a wrist, and pulled her to him. His pulse increased rapidly at the contact of her warm body.

Nona hauled off and struck at him with a balled fist. At first he looked surprised, then he laughed—a wild crazy laugh that somehow conveyed the idea that he had expected her to resist, and gloried in it.

The laugh stopped abruptly, however, when another blow hit

his cheek with a sound thud. He snarled suddenly and reached for her throat. It yielded softly under the pressure of his fingers.

But he released the pressure as quickly as he had applied it. The sudden fear which had leaped into her eyes stunned him. Somehow he knew that a woman could be expected to resist, but that it was rather a matter of form than anything else.

The horror which he had seen in her eyes a minute before was wrong. And now this terror—that was wrong, too. Abruptly he realized that he wanted this woman to like him, to welcome his attentions. She mustn't be afraid of him.

He released her entirely, letting his arms fall to his sides, a dumb look of hurt in his eyes.

"Mark," Nona whimpered, "what has happened to you? Why don't you know me? Why are you so old?"

CHAPTER XX

THE EXCHEQUER BLUES

SHE COVERED HER face with her hands and tried to get her thoughts in order. Things were happening too fast. The realization that the old man really was Mark had come to her the instant he had bent the cell door like a piece of wet spaghetti. No man could do that but Mark.

That thought had instantly brought to mind the cry she had thought she dreamed. That had been Mark's voice, astounded at the sight of her in the prison cell. It had resulted in giving the guard a chance to shoot him.

Then she knew what had happened. The streak of blue blood in his snowy hair proved it. The bullet had grooved along his skull, knocking him senseless. The remarkable healing power of his radio-active blood had restored the power to control his body, but his mind was still fogged.

The concussion had not had time to wear off. The brain was shocked, and had forgotten all it knew. Mark was like a primordial cave-man, conscious of his own existence, but governed almost entirely by instinct. Reason was present, of course, but knew no facts with which to reason.

The shock would wear off, and memory return, but that would take time. And there was no time. She would have to get him out of the prison. She mustn't wonder why her Mark was old or why he had come here. She would learn that when he recovered.

Nona, still sobbing from the shock to her own brain, placed a hand gently on the old man's arm.

The hurt look left Mark's eyes and he smiled. Then he grabbed her again, evidently satisfied that she had come around to his way of thinking. This time he was more gentle about it. But she pushed him away again.

He followed her when she left the cell and went into the one where he had killed the first man. He wondered briefly at the shudder she gave when she inadvertently looked at the distorted face of the man he had throttled.

Nor did he understand why she seemed to want the peculiar pieces of metal which she was trying to remove from their position under the man's body. Obligingly, he lifted the dead man off the key ring, by shoving a foot under the shoulder and pushing. The body thudded against the wall.

Nona retrieved the keys and tried one after another in the lock of Gladys' cell. Finally she found the right one and repeated the operation on the doors which confined Tolon and Forney.

Mark snarled a bit at the freeing of the others, but decided that they were friends of hers, and quieted down. He even contained himself when they led him out into a street filled with new people, all potential enemies.

Though possibly by this time he realized that other humans didn't necessarily have to be enemies, for no one showed any sign of wishing him harm.

By a circuitous route Tolon and Forney led the way back to headquarters.

DAYS WENT by with little clearing of Mark's mind. Attended solicitously by Nona, who shaved off his beard and removed the plastic skin which disguised him so effectively, he was quite content as long as she remained nearby.

The sight of Ira had momentarily given him a twinge of recollection, but it passed as quickly as it had come. Several times he experienced the same reaction when he saw familiar things or familiar faces, but his mind was not yet over the shock of the concussion, and the effect was fleeting.

The thieves had brought in the last of the caravan guards on the day of Mark's return. The one hundred and five which he had restored mentally helped to capture the others. The new captives were confined in a warehouse, for Mark had lost his power of hypnotism as thoroughly as he had lost his memory.

Ira anxiously awaited his recovery, for he had received information to the effect that Vargo was reorganizing his army and would shortly be able to go on with his plans for conquest. And while Ira was a capable leader and was taking effective measures to circumvent Vargo, he knew that without Mark there would be no permanent solution to the trouble.

In spite of the swelled ranks of the fraternity, they were having plenty of difficulty. It wasn't so easy to capture the new army leaders. Another trouble was the fact that Vargo's nobles were renewing their efforts to stamp out the rebellion.

He expected any moment to be raided. Sooner or later somebody would crack under the double threat of hypnotism and torture, and reveal the location of the hideout.

Several of the fraternity had been captured in the last few days. One of them might succumb. Ira took steps to prevent any more captures. He ordered that none of them engage in any thefts until further notice. The treasury would take care of all the expenses of its members until they could again forage for themselves.

He guessed from the evidence of Tolon and Forney that the nobles had been able to make their captures only by the expedient of placing apparently easy victims within the reach of the thieves. Bait, as Baron had called the process. When a thief struck, he found himself caught. The logical answer was for them to cease their larcenous activities and confine themselves to the capture of as many of the new army officers as possible.

Gladys, though she didn't want to at all, thought it her duty to return to her husband. Nona didn't have much trouble talking her out of it. Tolon wouldn't have allowed it anyway. He had been told of her plight, and had Nona's assurance that as soon as Mark regained his mind, he would take steps to annul the marriage.

Nona intended to help Mark in the reorganization of the city's life, taking on the job of ferreting out such couples as were hopelessly incompatible. Mark could free the minds of these people, and let them seek their own mates. Those who were living happily would be left in the state of hypnotic subjection which kept them together.

It would be ruinous to do otherwise. The years, children, and a dozen other considerations made it inadvisable to risk the results of completely freeing the majority of the people who had been hypnotized by Vargo. Much of his work had been a blessing, though he had never meant it that way.

Nona came to develop a real attachment for the people who made up the fraternity. Their loyalty to each other, and the idealistic faith they had in the justice of their motives, aroused her admiration. Thieves they might be, but Nona knew they weren't criminals at all.

In fact it was hard to say who were the real criminals. For the nobles were perfectly sincere in their desire to stamp out the menace to the plans of the great Vargo. They only acted as they did because of his hypnotic suggestion. The only real criminal was Vargo himself.

A WEEK passed and favorable reports came from the electrical experts concerning their work on the radio equipment. Progress had been quicker than they had expected.

Machines used for the manufacture of electric bulbs had been easily converted to the manufacture of radio tubes. Coils and condensers were simple to make. The apparatus was now ready to assemble and put in operation. Only a day or two would be required.

Mark had slept since the day of his accident—a thing he hadn't done for years. Several hours a day, when the others went to bed, he did likewise. Possibly the cause lay in the shocked condition of his brain, enabling him to revert to a habit he no longer needed. But whatever the cause, the result was as normal as Nona's deep slumber.

He awoke one evening, and looked up at the ceiling. For several minutes he lay there, gazing upward, trying to orient himself. He became conscious of someone beside him and turned his bead. It was Nona, of course, sleeping peacefully. That was all right, perfectly normal.

But he had been asleep also, and that wasn't normal. He wondered vaguely whether he had recaptured the ability, and went back to gazing at the ceiling. Then he became puzzled about its wallpaper design. Abruptly he realized that the Vikings didn't use wallpaper.

He sprang to his feet and looked out of a window. A dingy alley met his gaze. With the sight of it he remembered suddenly that he was no longer in Norway. He was in Detroit, and had an urgent task to perform!

Rigidly Mark stood at the window, as memory flooded back into his mind. In the space of seconds he reviewed all that had happened since Omega had dropped him in the ladies' shop. It came back vividly, as if he were viewing it on a motion picture screen. Even to the details which had happened since his brain had been shocked.

Smiling happily, he turned to face the bed. Nona's face was beautiful in repose, though as he watched her a frown passed fleetingly over it. Reaching over, he rumpled her hair. Her eyes opened and looked up at him in disbelief.

"You're back!" she breathed. "Mark!"

SEVERAL HOURS were required to bring Mark up to the present. Things had happened during the time his mind was fogged. He was tickled at the progress made by the electrical experts, and wanted to see them immediately. When they arrived he closeted himself with them for quite some time.

Ira fidgeted outside the conference chamber. There were a thousand things he wanted to talk over, and most of them were urgent. Disposition of the captured men was the greatest of his problems.

So many of Vargo's officers were prisoners of the fraternity that it was almost impossible to keep them confined any longer. A warehouse and several private homes were being used for the purpose, but because of the lack of proper facilities it was necessary to use a prohibitive number of the thieves to act as guards.

A point had been reached where no more could be captured because it would be impossible to hold them. Mark could solve the problem easily by hypnotizing the captives and making them members.

And even that was becoming a problem. The membership had reached a point where it was eating large holes in the treasury to support it. This, added to the feed bill of the prisoners, was rapidly bankrupting the fraternity. And there was nothing coming in!

Ira was in a decided dither, waiting to discuss plans with Mark. He didn't welcome Jan Thomas, who joined him in waiting at the door of the chamber, announcing that Mark would want to see him next.

"Who's boss around here?" Ira wanted to know.

"Mark," Thomas answered.

Ira nodded. "So he is," he said, looking a bit mystified as he realized that such was the case. He frowned at the guinea pig that Thomas held cradled in one arm.

Jan Thomas smiled enigmatically, but said nothing.

Eventually the experts trooped from the room. As before, they wore eager expressions as if they could hardly wait until they got to work at the thing which Mark had discussed with them. Ira pushed past Jan Thomas and entered the room. He tried to slam the door but the smaller man was too quick for him. And then too, Ira had to open the door wide to permit the passage of his own huge body. Thomas went in and darted around him to present the guinea pig to Mark.

"We've got it!" he cried, almost throwing the little beast at Mark. "The analysis was—"

"Mark!" interrupted Ira. "There are more important matters to be taken care of. You've got to—"

"Nonsense!" Thomas cried. "There's nothing more important than science."

It took some moments to quiet them, a thing which Mark accomplished by promising Ira to go immediately and take care of the captives, and while doing so to listen to the report of Thomas. The three set out for the warehouse where the majority of the prisoners were kept. The streets were dark and there was little danger of Mark being recognized.

Gently, as they left headquarters, he pressed the windpipe of the little animal. It didn't struggle, even when he closed off its supply of air completely. It just stopped breathing, as if it were only doing it to keep in practice anyway.

"THE ANALYSIS was easy," Thomas told him. "We killed quite a few pigs, however, before we found the proper concentrations to change the blood of a living animal as this one is changed."

"Does its present blood correspond with the sample, I gave you?"

"Precisely," Thomas informed. "Not the slightest difference. We've noticed some peculiar things, however. The beast doesn't eat. And it's slept only once in the past four days."

Mark nodded. "You've got it then," he said. "I don't eat either. I thought you knew that. The radio-activity supplies the energy normally furnished by the consumption of food. Sleep isn't necessary because lactic acid doesn't form. Did you try tiring the animal out?"

"Didn't think of it," said Thomas. "Don't tell me it won't tire!"

Mark shook his head. "Tiring is caused when physical exertion burns up energy faster than food and oxygen can replace it. This blue blood is able to supply energy from the slow breaking down of its radioactive element, faster than the body can burn it. The excess radiates away. And the element has a half-period, as you are aware, of more than ten thousand years."

Jan Thomas stopped dead in his tracks. For a second Mark thought he was going to faint. Ira solicitously extended a steadying hand. But Thomas didn't faint.

"Immortality!" he breathed. "The dream of man for ages!"

"Not quite," said Mark, smiling, "The organism will die as the concentration gets down to about a quarter strength. At least, so I've been told."

"But man! Think what it would mean if everyone had this blood. The earth wouldn't be able to support the population in a matter of a few decades!"

"You forget that food isn't necessary. Not even air. Only water. But don't worry about it. Only a very choice few will be given the injections. Those who will work for the betterment of themselves and humanity as a whole. That is a sort of a trust I must keep. There won't be any crowding for thousands of years to come. Perhaps never."

It was significant that neither Thomas nor Ira said a word of suggestion concerning who might be worthy of the new blood. Men of lesser character would have immediately suggested themselves. But both men realized that the matter lay in Mark's hands entirely, and that nothing they might say would influence him in the least.

THE WAREHOUSE was reached, and almost two hundred men were treated hypnotically to erase the suggestions of Vargo. They left as free men, only slightly under the influence of Mark's counter-suggestions. These were of a benign nature and would tend to nullify any natural hankering that any of the men might have in the direction of a war of conquest.

Several private homes, temporarily serving as prisons, were next on the program. When the last call was made the fraternity had swelled until it numbered slightly over four hundred.

Back once more at headquarters, Mark closeted himself with

Ira. The chief of the fraternity immediately went into a description of his many woes.

"… But the worst thing of all," he concluded, "is the shortage of funds. We can't go on any longer than another week, unless I send our men out to steal. And if I do, some will be caught. I had hoped—"

Mark caught at the hesitation. "Hoped what?" he prompted.

"I'd hoped that this thing would be settled before it became necessary to steal again," he answered. "As you know, we steal because we must survive, not because we want to. Every man of the fraternity has a legitimate profession he would rather follow, but refuses as long as he must work under Vargo. Can't we get this thing finished soon?"

Mark scratched his chin. "A week…."

"There's also the matter of the men he's captured," Ira interrupted. "Any day now one of them might crack, and we'll be wiped out. There's nowhere we can go, or I'd change headquarters. But right now we're so financially crippled that we can't rent new quarters."

Mark frowned. "That's next on the program," he said, thoughtfully. "And maybe I can do something about Vargo at the same time. Hold the fort till I get back."

CHAPTER XXI

POOSH 'EM UP, MARK

MARK EASED HIMSELF cautiously through the window in the upper story of the prison. He had approached just as warily, half expected to find a trap. But neither the outside nor the inside of the place showed any sign of one.

The bars he had ripped from the window were still lying where he had left them, and the only footprints in the dust on the corridor floor were his own and those of the guard.

Could it be that Vargo didn't know that he had once gained admittance to the prison?

Abruptly he realized that such could very well be the case. He had killed the guard, and if he remembered correctly the stone door which opened on the lower corridor had been closed when they left the prison. Vargo and his nobles probably thought that either Tolon or Forney had managed to get out of his cell and liberated the others.

There was no evidence that Mark had been there at all. The guard's broken neck and the mangled cell door might be puzzling them considerably, but that still didn't point in Mark's direction.

For Vargo and his henchmen didn't know of his extraordinary strength. The only other time he had used it since coming to the city, had been when he had bent the cell doors in releasing himself and Dodd. And that time he had hypnotized the guards and made them forget they had ever seen him.

Those conclusions, while reassuring, didn't prevent him from exercising the utmost caution in reaching the lower cell corridor. He didn't walk; he floated. Even the light patter of his sandals might be heard.

He smiled inwardly, realizing that he had forgotten his ability to soar, on the other occasion when he had come down these stairs. Even if he had remembered, the screech of the rusty-hinged doors at each landing would have nullified his own silence.

This time the doors were all open, and his descent was utterly without sound.

As a testimonial to his memory, the stone door at the bottom of the last flight was shut. As before, a thin crack of light lined its lower edge. Mark paused, trying to visualize the corridor behind that door. As he did so, he heard a voice. "Raise you two," it said.

"Check," said another.

"I'll see 'em," said still another. "Damn this hat!"

"My pot," claimed the first voice. "Say. Do you really think Vargo ordered these helmets?"

"That's what the captain said," was the answer.

"Yeah. But he'd rather lie than tell the truth. Remember the time he said it was Vargo's orders for us to take a bath once a day?"

"Do I remember? Say, I took seven baths before I found out it was just his idea of a joke. It's a good thing I found out when I did. That perfumed soap he issued was getting me in a lot of fights."

THERE WAS silence for a space, except for the slapping of cards being dealt. Mark felt a swift elation as the import of the men's words struck home.

His theory was confirmed. Vargo's hypnotic control of his subjects was powerful, so powerful that his words received obedience even when relayed through a second person. These men were wearing their helmets because their captain had said that Vargo had commanded it. Their minds were so conditioned that any order coming from him would be obeyed, as long as it was relayed by someone in authority.

The trouble here seemed to be that the captain was given to practical joking, and his word was therefore doubted. But they wouldn't hesitate an instant if Vargo's voice had issued the order. That was the important thing. Vargo, speaking over a radio, would be instantly and unquestionably obeyed. His voice alone would sway the thoughts, even the emotions of his people.

Mark stayed behind the door, hoping that the subject of the helmets would be reopened. It was.

"Suppose," postulated the first man, "that the captain is pulling another one of his jokes? There don't seem to be any good reason for wearing these things. I'd rather have my old one. This thing wouldn't stop a sword, let alone a bullet."

Another short silence. Then: "I'd hate to do anything against Vargo's orders. Maybe he has some reason for wanting us to wear them. I've noticed 'em on several of the nobles."

"Sure," said the first man. "Everybody in the palace has them. But I figure that's only to identify those who belong in the palace. Makes it easy to spot an outsider. And I figure that the order to keep them on at all times is one of the captain's inventions. They're terrible hot in this weather, and he gets a kick out of seeing us suffer. Gimme two cards."

"Make mine three," said the other man. "What are you going to do about it?"

"I'll take the thing off—that is, if you guys will. Nobody'll see us in here."

Mark held his breath—which he didn't need anyway—during the tense silence which followed. If the man's suggestion was taken up, his immediate problem would be solved. If it wasn't, he'd never be able to free the members of the fraternity who were imprisoned within.

The guards were at the far end of the corridor, too far away to risk rushing them. He'd collect too many slugs in the attempt.

"Suppose—"

"Rats with supposing! I'm taking mine off! If the captain hears about it, I'll know who told."

Mark heard the plunk of the helmet striking the floor. A second later it was followed by two more.

"Aaah. That's better."

Mark pulled the door open and stepped into the corridor. "Much better," he agreed, freezing the surprised three in their seats. "Go on with your game, boys. Don't think of anything else, least of all your prisoners."

Obediently, the three guards lost themselves in the game of cards, paying not the slightest attention when he removed the ring of keys from the wall. Nor did they turn their heads when he opened cell after cell, calling softly to the sleeping prisoners to get out and report back to Ira.

THE THIEVES came out of their cells, one by one, looked wonderingly at the guards, and quietly filed out the front door. Mark released the last one and shut the door after him.

Noticing that the card game seemed about to come to an abrupt end because one of the guards had garnered almost all of the visible cash, he reached over and redistributed it. Then he went on exploring.

Ira had said that a passage existed between this place and

the palace. The appearance of Dene Baron, the last time he was here, indicated the same thing. He certainly hadn't come in the door, for Mark had heard him come, even though he was barely conscious and trying to regain his senses at the time.

A few minute's search showed him the entrance to the tunnel. It was at the other end of the corridor, and protected by a locked door of thick iron bars. One of the keys on the ring opened it.

Once more resorting to his gift of levitation, Mark floated along the tunnel. It was dark and he proceeded slowly. Even so, he failed to stop himself when it abruptly branched off to the right. He fetched up with a thud against the wall.

The new course became lighter, the further he progressed. Dimly he could see another turn, around which there was a light burning. Its rays were reflected from the wall and gave him light enough to prevent another bump.

The tunnel ended in a flight of stairs. Silently Mark floated up. There was a door at the top—an ordinary door, not a barred, iron one. Carefully he opened it, and found, surprisingly, an elevator shaft.

There wasn't any car, and the shaft was so dark that he couldn't see where it might be. One thing was certain: the car was at an upper floor. It couldn't be lower, for the bottom of the shaft was at the stair landing.

But how far up, he could only guess. There was nothing to do but go up and find out. Slowly, hoping that nobody would decide to come down, he ascended the shaft.

GRUDGINGLY HE gave Vargo credit for the forethought which had planned this avenue from the palace to the prison. Except when the cage was at the bottom of the shaft, there was no possibility that anyone would use it as a means of escaping from the prison itself.

Nor did it provide a means of ingress into the palace for any body of invaders who might be able to capture the prison. The height he traveled before his outstretched hands came in contact with the bottom of the car would have made it impossible for an ordinary man to climb. The cables were thick with grease and wouldn't provide a hand-hold.

Nor was there an opening at any of the lower floors. Mark estimated that the car was resting at the very top floor of the palace.

Gropingly he explored the bottom of the car. There was no opening in it, nor were there any cracks which might indicate the presence of a trapdoor. Similarly, there was nothing but smooth concrete on all sides of the shaft. How was he to get out?

There was a door, he knew, at the level of the car; though he couldn't guess which side of the shaft it was on. He'd turned around so many times that his sense of direction was all out of gear. But knowing wouldn't have helped any, for he couldn't reach it.

Several minutes passed while he thought the problem out. Then he placed a hand on the side of the shaft, to make certain that he held himself in one position, and brought all the power of his mind into the effort of moving the elevator cage.

Telekinesis would solve the problem, if big control proved itself versatile enough for the job. There would almost certainly be a space in the shaft above the car. He must manipulate the energy waves which surged about him, and make them do two things at the same time.

One of these things they were already doing: the task of holding him without other support at a spot over a hundred feet above the bottom of the shaft. But the second manipulation was of proportions far greater than anything he had tried up to the present.

The car was heavy, and a terrific concentration of the waves would be required to lift it. Yet the energy waves were abundant, and it shouldn't be any harder to make them perform this task than it was to make them carry a quantity of air with him when he flew. The mental gymnastic involved differed only in degree.

Mark applied himself with confidence. The feel of the flowing but resistless waves of energy became intense, almost tangible.

The tips of the fingers of his left hand rested against the bottom of the cage. As he increased the pressure of the waves, he felt it move, slowly and ponderously, upward. He moved his right hand to a higher position on the wall, and let his body follow upward.

In the total darkness there was no other way of gauging his progress. He avoided exerting too much pressure on the moving car, for fear the energy at his command might slam it through the roof of the palace. He was juggling with cosmic forces, and must treat them with respect.

With light, the task would have been easier, but as it was he must check himself with the sense of touch.

But even that little maneuver of hitching himself upward required a delicate balance of the waves. Entirely by mental control he held the car motionless, bunching the energy against it while he advanced his body to a new position.

The energy which held the car mustn't be confused with that which lifted his body, either. If that should happen, even for the slightest instant, he would be dashed to a smear against its bottom. The two flows of energy must be carefully kept separate, each doing its appointed task.

Slowly the car moved upward. Then he stopped it and took another hitch. But this time, as he delicately fed more power to the waves of energy pressing against the car, it remained at rest. Carefully he increased the pressure. The car still didn't move!

Puzzled for an instant, he held the power as it was. Then he decided that his perception of the energy waves was slightly imperfect, and that he really wasn't exerting as much as he thought. Accordingly he exerted still more.

Abruptly there was a rending, tearing roar of twisted girders and shattered masonry. The car had pushed itself through the top of the shaft!

INSTANTLY REALIZING what had happened, Mark relaxed the pressure, holding the car stationary. A moment of panic now would be fatal. If he forgot for a second the mass of weight which hovered over his head, it would fall and crush him.

But his control was perfect; not even a scrap of the shattered concrete fell into the shaft.

He was no longer in darkness now. A thin crack of light outlined a door on the other side of the shaft, opposite to and slightly higher than his present position. Cautiously he moved toward it, keeping one half of his mind on the energy which supported the elevator cage.

Fumblingly, fearful of losing his control, he groped for the door's fastenings.

There was no room in his mind for the possible commotion which the sound of the crash might be causing in the palace beyond that door. He didn't think of the inmates who might be searching for the source of the sound; of the armed guards which would be swarming the corridors of the palace. His mind was completely occupied with the task at hand.

If there had been the slightest amount of reasoning power left for him to command he would have retreated, leaving the elevator cage to dangle at the end of its cables.

But there wasn't. He was irrevocably committed to a course of action; the course he had planned before his mind had become too occupied with the manipulation of cosmic energies to leave room for other things. That plan of action had included the opening of the door as soon as he raised the car enough to permit it. And open the door he did.

The inner latch operated by a lever, and his groping hand discovered it. The door slid back. People were moving along the corridor—soldiers, nobles, and palace menials. All wore the helmets which protected them from hypnotism.

But Mark saw none of them. They passed before his eyes as fleeting shadows, not even impressing the brain behind those eyes. That brain was filled with the necessity of moving himself through the doorway and at the same time keeping the elevator cage from dashing down upon his unprotected skull.

The instant his feet came to rest upon the corridor floor, he released the pressure which was supporting the car. It fell, pausing only slightly when the cables stretched and parted; then crashed with a deafening din at the bottom of the shaft.

As if the sound released his mind from the fetters which had held it, he became aware of the scene before him. A dozen pop-eyed soldiers had him covered with pistols. They were infinitely more astounded than he, for as soon as he saw them he realized that the sound of the car going through the roof must have awakened everybody in the palace.

But that fact didn't help him in the least. Their guns were centered on his body and there were too many to ignore.

A noble appeared on the scene and took charge. He was as mystified as any of the soldiers concerning the real nature of the things which had happened; but he had a better grip on his nerves. He ordered them to conduct Mark down the corridor.

The party stopped before a massive oaken door. The noble rapped on it with his knuckles. A tiny slit opened at a level with his head, and a pair of suspicious eyes looked out.

"What do you want?" came the muffled growl.

"Tell Vargo we've captured a prisoner at the top of the elevator shaft," said the noble. "The noise was apparently caused when the cage crashed at the bottom of the shaft. If there were any others, they went down with it. We caught only one."

"Let me see him," said the guard.

The noble stepped back. The eyes roved over Mark and then suddenly disappeared from the slit. In a minute the massive door swung wide.

"Just him," said the guard, training his pistol on Mark's stomach. "The rest of you stay out."

CHAPTER XXII

MEET MR. MOUSE

VARGO, IN SILK nightclothes, sat on a heavily upholstered chair beside an ornate bed. The covers on the bed were rumpled as if he had recently jumped out of it.

A dozen other chairs were in the room; hard ones and not designed for comfort. Mark supposed that these were for the twelve brawny guards who were watching him alertly. Vargo probably slept with them in the room.

Vargo regarded him through slitted eyes. His face, evilly repulsive, was wrinkled and parchment-dry. The gayly colored silk failed to conceal the scrawny body of the aged ruler. Mark received an impression of the man which amplified the one he got on the occasion of their last meeting. An old man, incredibly evil and self-centered.

Then abruptly Vargo smiled. His face took on a benevolence which Mark would have said was impossible only a moment before. It was clothed with an expression of friendly welcome, both cordial and reassuring—to anybody who hadn't seen the other expression.

"I'm certainly glad to see you," he said, his cracked voice filled with relief. "It's a pleasure, a rare pleasure."

"Nice of you to say so," Mark replied. "I'd figured this meeting out a little differently."

Vargo beamed. "With my hat off, eh? Sorry I can't oblige. But I've cultivated an affection for this hat. I'll keep it on."

"I was afraid of that," Mark confessed. "Well, what's next on the program? You ordered me shot, once before."

Vargo nodded amiably. "Silly, wasn't it?" he said. "But I countermanded that order. I knew you'd come here sooner or later, since you said you wanted my form of government changed. So I put my Ancestors to work devising this helmet. Everybody in the palace must wear one. Ingenious things, aren't they?"

"Why did you change the orders?" Mark asked, though he could already guess the answer.

Vargo shook a finger chidingly. "Don't be coy," he said. "You've got something I don't have. You can teach me. I'd like to fly like you do."

Mark grinned sardonically. "After which, of course, you'll set me free."

Vargo's expression remained affable. "No," he drawled. "But there are several ways of dying. Your reward for proper cooperation will be a quick one. Need I elaborate?"

"No," Mark said. "Your droolings aren't very entertaining. And it will be impossible to teach you to fly, so you might as well think up an appropriate way to kill me."

Vargo's face clouded. "Impossible? How?"

"There is only one way you could be made to sense the waves of energy which make flying possible. That way is to submit to my hypnosis. And of course you're afraid to do that."

VARGO BIT his lips nervously. He looked aimlessly about the room, his eyes resting momentarily on each of the guards, as if he half expected some comment from them. Then his eyes returned suddenly to Mark.

Instantly Mark felt the impact of Vargo's hypnosis wave. For a second it beat back his will, and waves of blackness hammered at his brain. Then his own powers rescued him, and the waves receded.

"You didn't suspect this was a one-way affair, this helmet," Vargo said, wearily. "An electrical unit in the collar provides the field which shields my brain; but my own wave cuts it off allowing me to hypnotize at will. It turns itself on automatically as soon as my wave ceases."

"It didn't do you much good, did it?"

"Harrumph!" said Vargo. "Of course it did, young man. You went down—well, a *little* anyhow. And I learned that you were bluffing. You can teach me your ability without hypnotism."

For a second Mark believed him. The waves of blackness *had* engulfed him for a brief instant.

But then the inconsistency of Vargo's statement struck him. True, he couldn't give Vargo the power of telekinesis by hypnotism. But neither could he give it to him any other way. Omega had operated on that part of his brain which controlled the faculty before he had been able to use it.

And he hadn't the slightest notion how to duplicate the operation.

Mark smiled indulgently. "You flatter yourself," he told Vargo. "You aren't strong enough to put me down."

The king's face twisted in rage. Mark smiled at the contortion, and that only served to make it worse. Vargo went white and began to tremble.

Then suddenly he seemed to regain control of himself. In the space of a few seconds he changed from a man on the verge of an apoplectic stroke to the kindly, benevolent old fellow he had been a few minutes ago.

"I'll submit to your hypnosis," he finally said. "And you'll teach me to fly; nothing else!" Vargo broke off and fell to chuckling evilly. It was some minutes before he said anything coherent. "The great Vargo can see to that. Do you want to know how?"

"How?"

Vargo fell into another fit of chuckling.

"Simple. Oh, so terribly simple. I should have thought of it sooner. First you shall be hypnotized!

"Don't smile. You can be hypnotized. There are twenty trained hypnotists on my Vocation Board. Once I placed two of them *en rapport* in the course of an experiment. They were able to put down the resistance of a third man by combining their power. And that man was very strong, too.

"Tomorrow I will place all twenty of them *en rapport*. Together, they will break your resistance. Then, while under their power, you will teach me to fly. In fact, you'll teach me all you know. Take him away!"

MARK WAS a very worried man when he was placed in a dungeon in the lowermost basement of the palace.

There were several good reasons for this. The most important was the fact that for once he found himself in a cell which seemed to be escape-proof—even for him it was a large affair, dimly lighted through a small, square hole in the heavy, stone door.

Entirely composed of granite, damp and cold, the cell would have held twenty people, and have held them until Doomsday. The heavy door would have withstood the battering of a pile-driver.

Mark had a notion that he could force the thing by utilizing the means which had pushed the elevator through the roof; but that was impractical. Guards placed at the ends of the passage-way outside his cell would be attracted by the noise and fill him with lead before he could get out.

Another reason for his mental turmoil was the fact that he didn't dare stay here and face the very real possibility that the twenty hypnotists of Vargo might overcome him. If they did, and learned that he had been bluffing, Vargo would cook his goose thoroughly.

Not only that, but they would learn all the plans of the fraternity as well. That would be the end of everything.

Angrily he paced back and forth in the cell, trying to think a way out of his difficulties.

But angry pacing, it seemed, wasn't conducive to clear thinking. He stopped, after a few moments, and made an intelligent survey of the cell. But that brought nothing, either. If was just as solid as before.

It was damnable.

The only thing he noticed that he hadn't seen before was a narrow crack which extended for a foot or so at the bottom of one wall. That didn't help a bit. It merely indicated that the monstrous slab of rock which formed that wall didn't fit quite as snugly as it might.

If this were above ground he might try to use the vast energy at his command to force the wall outward; but that would be senseless if solid earth was back of the stone. Even if he did force it silently, there would be no way out.

Absently he examined the door. It was solid and fitted like the case of a watch. He had seen the heavy iron bar which secured it on the outside and knew that there was no way of reaching it. The small hole was large enough to pass his arm through but was located too high to be of any use. His arm wouldn't be long enough to reach the bar.

Mark swore.

To think better he tried sitting down on the floor; gave that up because it was uncomfortably damp. His eyes happened on the crack in the opposite wall and he noticed that several roaches had decided to investigate his presence. At least there were quite a few of them on the floor near the crack, though of course they might only be searching for crumbs.

Quietly he crossed the cell and put an end to their existence. Mark didn't like roaches, even in dungeons. He stamped the life out of a dozen or two before the rest escaped into the crack. That, he hoped, would discourage any further exploration.

It didn't, as he noticed in a few minutes.

The next explorer wasn't a roach however. It was a mouse, small and clumsily fat. Mark scuffed a foot, expecting to see it dart back into the crack. The mouse only looked up, as if slightly startled, and regarded him insolently.

Then it approached one of the defunct roaches and hit it once with a paw. It repeated this operation haphazardly with several more; then, apparently decided that they weren't very good sport, and left them alone.

Next act of the mouse was to waddle closer to Mark and inspect him carefully. Finally he sniffed, as if contemptuous of a mere man, and went back to the roaches, smacking them around some more.

MARK WATCHED with interest, glad to give his mind a brief rest from its many problems. Suddenly he noticed that the dead roaches were apparently falling into a pattern as the mouse pushed them around.

He took a step closer to make sure that the dim light wasn't playing tricks on his eyes. The mouse paid no attention, other than to sniff irritatingly.

Sure enough, a dozen or so of the roaches were arranged so as to form two letters of the alphabet—D and O. Roughly, to be sure, and probably accidentally; but Mark nevertheless watched closely to see if the mouse did anything else significant.

But apparently he didn't intend to do so. He looked up at Mark as if to say that he didn't think much of the human race in general, for he raised his head in a disdainful manner and sniffed again, this time pointedly. Then he resumed his game, wrecking the two letters he had formed.

Mark was about to give him a swift kick in the place where his pants would be if he wore any, when he suddenly noticed that the mouse had formed more patterns. Letters again—this time a P and an E. Once more interested, Mark watched closely. But the mouse quit his game and sat up on his hind legs as if waiting for applause.

Suddenly Mark swore. It had occurred to him that the four letters spelled a word, and a darned appropriate one at that.

"All right, toots," he growled. "I know you're not a man, but you don't have to be a mouse, either.

"Omega," Mark said.

At this recognition of his peculiar talents, the mouse swelled pridefully. In fact, he continued to swell. In the twinkling of an eye he reached the size of a man, Then he melted a bit around the edges and actually became a man—the aged one which Omega delighted in being.

"But you're a dope," he said, amiably. "Any way you look at it. You let Vargo beat you again. The trouble is that you refuse to utilize your powers. You have a brain and you don't use it. You have telekinesis, and you don't use that, either. You could have licked him easily. You could have dropped the roof on him."

Mark shook his head. "As a last resort maybe," he admitted. "But I want him alive. I want to hypnotize him and make him spend the rest of his life correcting the wrongs he's committed. Once I get a chance to hypnotize him, I'll make him a model citizen, interested in the people's welfare and anxious to do what's right by them. I'll put his genius to good use.

"Then I'll release the Ancestors. They'll be glad to undo some of the work they've done in the past thirty years. For one thing, they should be able to do something about the growth ray. They'll have to find some way of making it harmless to the men who operate it.

"There's a hundred things to be done, and they hinge, for the most part, on keeping Vargo alive."

Omega nodded. "Good idea. You do use your brain, after all. But not as much as you might. Telekinesis, for instance. It could get you out of this cell."

"How?"

"Lots of ways. Think it out for yourself. I just dropped in to bawl you out, not to help you. Don't you think I have other things to do?"

Mark frowned, quite exasperated, for Omega's "other things" didn't seem nearly as important as getting out of this dungeon.

THE OLD man faded slightly and turned into a beautiful flower girl, complete with a basket of flowers, which she proceeded to toss gayly about as she danced lightly over the damp floor. The lighthearted tune which she sang to accompany her dance had a lyric which would have blistered the ears of a caravan driver. It furnished, in fact, such a sour note to an otherwise perfect performance that Mark had difficulty concentrating on a way to use telekinesis to get out of the cell.

And he knew very well that Omega intended to stick around until he solved the problem.

He did, however, hit upon an idea. Omega had told him that he would have to teach himself the many things which could be done with the power, aside from the most simple one of moving matter by means of the waves.

Creation of matter was one of the biggest uses of the energy. Destruction of matter was another. If he could use that one, he could dissolve the iron bar which held the door. But could he do it?

He decided to try. It seemed to be the only solution.

The bar was iron; of that he was sure. He had seen the rust on it. Thinking back to his early, and skimpy, study of physics he tried to visualize the atomic structure of the element. The atomic weight, he remembered, was about fifty-five.

He also remembered having seen a diagram of the probable molecular arrangement of iron. The problem was to use the energy waves at his disposal to cause the bar to dissolve or change into something else. He couldn't release the stored-up energy of the atoms or the explosion would bring down the entire palace.

Vainly he wished he knew the process which he'd seen Omega use so many times. The things he caused to vanish, did just that, probably dissipating their energy into the fourth dimension or something.

Omega didn't aid his mental processes in the least. Tiring of his flower girl act, he had decided to do something more sinister in nature. A gory fight between a pair of spiders and a cobra was the result of his effort. Mark shut his eyes and tried to concentrate.

Finally he hit upon the solution of his problem. Since he

couldn't attempt to turn the iron into pure energy, for obvious reasons, and since he didn't know enough to transmute it into something else, he'd try to melt it!

He had the means, if he could direct the energy waves in the proper manner. Energy makes heat when applied in many ways. Friction is one way, but that wouldn't do here. He had to create intense heat if he wanted to melt iron.

Why not use the energy directly, causing the atoms to speed up their motion?

MARK BECAME so engrossed in the problem that he didn't notice at all when the carcasses of the cobra and the two spiders vanished—the fight had ended in a draw—and were replaced by two colonies of ants, one black and one red, which immediately formed in battle array. Nor did he see the conflict which followed, led by miniature fife and drum corps on both sides.

He was too busy concentrating and directing energy waves to do things which were new to him. A dozen times he tried before he finally hit upon the proper method of directing the waves. When he did, the bar on the outside of the door glowed, became incandescent and slowly dripped on the floor.

He continued until he could no longer hear the drips; then he sighed and turned to Omega. That individual, he saw, had turned himself into a python, tied himself in a knot, and was vainly trying to untie himself. He gave up and returned to the guise of the aged man.

"Very clever," he applauded. "You've mastered something new. But why didn't you do the obvious thing, and lift the bar from its sockets?"

"I couldn't," Mark defended. "My arm isn't long enough."

"Oh," said, Omega, scratching his chin judiciously. "It was your arm then, which lifted that elevator?"

Mark flushed.

"I forgot," he confessed. "I couldn't see it, and it didn't occur to me that the waves would act through the door. But anyway, I did something new. Now suppose you tell me some of the other ways I could use telekinesis to get out of here. You said there were several."

"Come over here," said Omega, and placed one hand down near the crack under the wall.

Mark did likewise and felt a draft. That meant that there was air beyond the wall, and not earth. Abruptly he slammed all the energy he could muster against it. The slab of granite was pushed outward, breaking in half as it fell with a crash. There was another dungeon on the other side. He jumped through and headed for the open door.

AT HIGH speed he traversed the corridor outside, and ascended a flight of stairs. Omega, chuckling loudly, floated beside him. Two startled guards took potshots at them when they reached the top, but neither slowed in the slightest.

Mark was traveling at express-train speed toward a window, which he crashed through without bothering to open. Outside, he soared high above the grove of trees on the palace grounds. The rush of the wind felt good after the dankness of the underground cell. Omega kept pace, once more humming the song of the flower girl.

"Thanks, old smelt," Mark said, when they were well out of shooting distance.

"Don't mention it," said Omega, graciously. "Have you made up your mind yet?"

"What about? Oh, you mean the matter of descendants?"

"What else, dope?"

"I wish you'd quit calling me a dope. First thing you know I'll be believing it."

"The sooner the better. But that's not answering my question."

"No. To tell you the truth, I've been so busy I haven't thought about it at all."

Mark quaked inwardly as Omega appeared to be thinking it over. He was afraid his mentor would ask for an immediate decision, and thus force the issue. And he didn't want to reveal his own plans until they were well under way.

"Well"—Omega finally broke the silence—"don't wait too long. The next time I drop in, I'd like to know what you're going to do about it. So long." Mark thought he heard a disembodied chuckled float eerily back to him after Omega vanished, but the sound was so faint that he couldn't be sure.

He sped toward headquarters. There were a thousand things to be done and he had only a week in which to do them. Vargo would have to be licked. Well, the radio idea was still good. There would have to be a few refinements....

CHAPTER XXIII

AMATEUR NIGHT

ACTIVITY DURING THE next few days was furious. Mark visited the factories where the electrical experts were employed. He had them introduce him to the chiefs of the various plants. Without warning he hypnotized each of these, and left them with certain post-hypnotic suggestions.

Ira he trained for a part in his plan. Tolon also he coached. Gladys and Nona were given parts to perform. Everyone worked like a beaver to make himself letter-perfect in the parts to be played.

Announcements were sent out, as a result of Mark's hypnotism, by the various officials of the electrical companies. The wonders of radio transmission were explained. The announcement stated that every citizen of Detroit who applied to one of the companies would be given a ticket for a seat in one of the receiving auditoriums on the day of the initial broadcast.

Glowing descriptions of the type of entertainment to be offered was included in the announcements. The many uses of radio were explained, not even skipping its military value. Mark included this last because he wanted every citizen to attend, and war was of paramount interest at the present. It also was meant to be a lure for Vargo.

Vargo himself was sent a special invitation to broadcast personally. The presidents of the companies involved delivered the invitations themselves. They did so in accordance to Mark's suggestion, and dwelt upon the advantage to a ruler of being able to speak to all of his subjects whenever he wished. They told him that the receivers were inexpensive and could be installed in every home. The military value of radio was also impressed upon him, though it appeared that Vargo was more interested in the first virtue of this new wonder.

He accepted, promising to prepare a speech for the occasion.

When the fraternity was notified of his acceptance there was a certain amount of subdued rejoicing at headquarters. That was the first stumbling block in Mark's plan, and it had been hurdled. He hoped that the rest of the plan would work out as smoothly.

In the days of feverish preparation for the event, Mark became well acquainted with the people who were working with him. Jan Thomas, of course, could have no part in the proceedings. Nor could anyone who might be recognized by a member of Vargo's retinue. Tolon was one of these.

But both Tolon and Jan Thomas had work to do. For Mark had been watching both men, and had made up his mind about them. They were fine characters, however dissimilar.

Jan Thomas was a true scientist, one of the kind that had made the twentieth century one of the most progressive eras in the history of man. He worked assiduously for the pleasure of working, and with no thought of personal gain. An accomplishment was payment in itself for the grueling hours which had made it possible.

A fact learned or a fact proven, was worth all the gold in the world to Jan Thomas. In the days that followed the perfection of the serum, he hadn't once intimated that he himself was a worthy recipient of its miraculous virtues. Mark was convinced that the thought had never entered his head.

Tolon, an exact opposite of Thomas—young, virile, and filled with the joy of living—claimed Mark's attention also. For that young man had virtues all his own. An adventurous, rollicking spirit, he nevertheless had an ingrained sense of fairness and consideration for the rights of others.

Considering the nature of his recent employment, he was

an exemplary citizen. In spite of his grand contempt for the authority of Vargo, and the fact that he made his living as a thief, that was still true. For he believed in the equality of man and was willing to chance anything to bring about the freeing of the minds of the people of Detroit. Even in his thefts he had invariably picked victims who appeared prosperous enough to stand a slight loss.

MARK PUT Jan Thomas to work making a small supply of the serum. Enough to inject a half-dozen persons. He memorized the ingredients himself, for he wanted to know that formula for future use. Later he intended to subject Thomas to hypnotic suggestion and make him forget the formula.

Mark realized that in order to keep his trust he alone must judge those who were worthy of the injection. Omega's dream of a better world must come true. His own meddling mustn't shatter it, which would surely happen if the blessing were spread indiscriminately.

To make sure that the formula remained a secret, he hypnotized the two old scientists who had helped Thomas develop the serum. He erased all memory of the occurrence from their brains and substituted a fabricated memory to account for the days they had spent working on it.

To assist Thomas in the making of the serum, he pressed Tolon into service. His duties as an assistant didn't require technical knowledge, and the two worked well together. The supply of serum which Mark required was finished on the day before the great broadcast was to be made.

It was late in the afternoon when Mark sent for Tolon, Thomas, Ira and Gladys. He and Nona received them in the meeting room of the fraternity. Nona served drinks and Mark talked.

He told them of Omega and of the reason for Mark and Nona's difference in blood chemistry. To the best of his ability he outlined the idealism of Omega's experiment in human lives. He told them of the things which Omega didn't like about humans: their wars, their petty jealousies, and their selfishness.

As he talked, he scanned their faces and tried to penetrate their reactions. They satisfied him. He saw the wonder in their faces as he told them of Omega's existence and his nature. He saw their approval of his idealism.

"Now," he finished, "what do you think his reaction would be if I made several others like myself and Nona? Remembering, of course, that it is his wish that only our descendants form the new race which will some day be the only survivors of humanity."

They thought that over for a minute and then gave a diversity of answers. They ranged from the opinion that Omega would approve the action, to the guess that the disembodied intelligence would annihilate all such recipients of the blood, including Mark and Nona.

Mark grinned, admitting that their guess was as good as his. "Do you think that there are any humans living who would risk his anger, for the blessings which would be theirs after the injection, and for the honor of participating for the experiment?"

A clamor greeted that question. Everyone present, it seemed, would be glad to risk Omega's displeasure. And not only for the near immortality to themselves, but that their children would number among those favored of humans.

Mark looked at Nona. She nodded, her face aglow.

THE DECISION made, and by the ones who were most concerned, Mark wasted no time. Looking into Gladys' eyes, he separated her mind from all bodily sensation. A hypodermic needle injected its fluid into the veins of an arm.

He held her brain in the grip of his hypnosis wave for a full minute, giving the serum a chance to diffuse itself completely in the blood stream: The hypnosis was necessary to prevent the nerve shock which had placed him in suspended animation for six millennia. Omega had used the same nerve block when he had injected Nona.

In rapid succession he treated the others, leaving Tolon for last. When Tolon was snapped awake, he immediately gathered Gladys into his arms and tried to kiss her. She laughingly averted her face.

"After the annulment," she promised.

"That'll be automatic when I de-hypnotize your husband," Mark told her.

Tolon finished his kiss while she was thinking that one over.

"I don't feel any different," claimed Ira.

"You are," Mark assured him. "And don't get married unless you see me first. That goes for you too, Jan. Choose wisely, for I can't guarantee that I'll use these other doses unless you do."

Mark dismissed the four, suddenly feeling that he had crossed a fearful Rubicon. He was relieved that he had acted as he had, and that there was no turning back or changing his mind; but an obscure brain cell or two persisted in reminding him that there was almost certain to be a reckoning.

Nona, frankly jubilant that the problem was solved, had no such worries. Although Mark hadn't known it, Nona had been worried and mentally ill at ease for quite some time. The problem of the future of her children had bothered her even more than it had him. That is why there was no room in her mind for apprehension about the possible consequences of Mark's act.

The day of the broadcast found everybody concerned, eager to get it over. They were letter-perfect in their roles and rehearsals had been thorough; but none of them were trained entertainers and they suffered the usual stage-fright at the thought of their first performance.

Mark assured them that even the most practical entertainers would be similarly stricken at their first broadcast. Radio was something to disconcert the best of them at the first try.

Ira was to be master of ceremonies. The performers gathered in the anteroom of the improvised studio, a large soundproofed room in one of the electrical laboratories. Vargo was to have the feature spot on the program, and would witness the performances of all the others.

And though he didn't know it, Mark had prepared his speech for him. It would be a totally different thing from the speech he was planning to make. For Mark intended that the broadcast would end all the more vicious of the suggestions which Vargo had placed in the minds of his subjects, over so many years of his reign.

The speech, as Mark prepared it, would stop all desire for war. The voice of Vargo, which the people of Detroit were conditioned to obey, would preach a new set of ideals.

By messenger came the word that all the public auditoriums rented for the occasion were jammed to capacity. Several outdoor meeting places had been equipped with receivers and amplifiers to take care of the overflow. The attendance exceeded all expectations.

Mark would have been satisfied to broadcast to a majority of the population. That would have served his purpose.

But Vargo had been sold completely by the idea of again exerting his influence upon people he hadn't seen since their appearance before the Vocation Board, and had ordered every citizen who was physically able to attend the broadcast. As a result about ninety-seven per cent of the population were anxiously awaiting the broadcast.

VARGO HADN'T as yet made his appearance. The performers began to fidget, Ira himself leading the fidgeting. He was probably the most nervous of all. For upon him rested the responsibility of getting Vargo to remove his shielding helmet. Mark had concealed himself in a cabinet not far from the microphone. It was marked conspicuously, *DANGER—10,000 VOLTS.*

He didn't dare let himself be seen by Vargo before the helmet was removed. And he was certain that the king would be adequately surrounded by a bodyguard, so that he would get no chance to snatch it off. He had thought of doing that, but realized that even if he did manage to remove the shield he would be punctured by a dozen bullets before he could break down Vargo's not inconsiderable resistance. Ira would have to do the job.

There was a narrow slot in the cabinet, at a level with Mark's eyes and facing the microphone. A piece of smoked glass prevented anyone from penetrating the darkness within. Mark could remove it when the proper time came. Heavily insulated wires led from the top of the cabinet to give credence to the danger sign.

He was sure nobody would investigate its contents. People were very cautious about running the risk of grabbing a handful of volts.

Vargo arrived finally, with heavy dramatic accompaniment. A platoon of soldiers, all wearing the new helmets, came first. They went through the broadcasting rooms with a fine-toothed comb.

Those of the men who carried pistols were relieved of them. Closets and lockers were investigated for hidden assassins, though all of the soldiers shied away from Mark's cabinet.

Then the platoon arranged itself along the wall of the studio, and a man blew a whistle. Vargo, surrounded by a bodyguard of ten men, answered the blast. He marched in, smiling benignly, and accepted an upholstered chair from Ira, who placed it several feet from the microphone and directly opposite Mark's cabinet.

Nona was the first performer. She came in at Ira's signal, and curtsied to Vargo. Then she approached the microphone, and as she did so a thin squeal was heard, gaining in volume as she came closer. Ira halted her apologetically.

"There must be some metal among your garments," he said. "The microphone is very sensitive to metals."

Nona removed a brooch from the neckpiece of her dress, and handed it to him. He carried it away from the microphone and the squealing ceased. Vargo and his soldiers watched the byplay, though they had no way of knowing that Mark was causing the squeal by turning a rheostat inside his cabinet.

IRA MADE an announcement, and Nona sang. Her throaty voice, singing a Viking folk song, enchanted all who listened.

She finished, curtsied again, retrieved her brooch, and left the studio.

A comedy team was next, and a loud squeal greeted their approach. Ira explained again the peculiar effect of metals in close proximity to the microphone. They, were obliged to remove coins and belt buckles and leave them on the other side of the studio.

The two were nervous at first, but soon forgot it, and drew a big hand from the king's soldiers. Vargo himself applauded heartily. He seemed very much pleased with the performance.

Act after act went through without a hitch. Gladys sang a popular song, and the male quartet sang a slightly bawdy marching song of the caravan guards. This drew the greatest applause from the king's soldiers, though none of the acts failed to get some appreciation.

The last performance, a duet starring Nona and Gladys, concluded the fraternity's part of the program. Next was to be the speech by Vargo. His bodyguard approached the microphone with him. The squeal which greeted them was deafening.

Ira was extremely apologetic as he pointed out that their guns and swords were metallic. Vargo frowned and then issued terse orders. The pianist was hustled from the room. Ira, the only remaining person who wasn't among Vargo's retinue, found himself covered by a dozen guns.

Vargo approached the microphone again. A thin squeal, rising in pitch and volume was the result. Vargo stepped back. He examined his clothing and removed a belt buckle. The squeal came again when he neared the microphone. He stepped back again and faced Ira.

"Make an announcement," he directed. "Say that Vargo, Giver of Life, will speak to his people after a short pause. All listeners are to remain and wait."

Ira did as he was ordered, suppressing his nervousness, and masking all emotion behind his inscrutable poker face.

"Now," said Vargo. "You were about to suggest that my helmet might contain some metal, weren't you?"

Ira paled, though his face wore an apologetic smile. "There must be some metal about the person of your majesty. The microphone only acts like that in the presence of metal."

Vargo's eyes gleamed. "Have you ever looked in a mirror, my traitorous friend?" he asked. "Try it some time, and notice particularly the gleaming gold inlays in your teeth."

Mark groaned inaudibly, cursing himself for a fool. He hadn't even thought of Ira's teeth, which should have caused quite a squeal. Nona's gold brooch should have been left on to explain that gold was the one metal which didn't affect the microphone. Vargo, an intelligence of the first order, had seen the inconsistency.

But there was still a chance to win. Mark quickly removed the smoked glass from his peep-hole. No one was looking toward the cabinet, he had a few moments in which to work. Before, Vargo would order a more complete search of the studio and the surrounding rooms.

He had probably already reasoned the motive behind the attempted removal of the helmet. There was only one man who could possibly want that helmet removed.

CHAPTER XXIV

MAY I CUT IN?

GATHERING ALL HIS mental perception of the energy waves about him, Mark concentrated on the helmet. Lead was the metal: 207.10 to 207.22 in atomic weight. Exerting every ounce of energy, he concentrated on the helmet.

Silver might also be present, in minute quantity; for lead extracted from galena—the usual source—always contains it. To be certain of success, he must provide for it.

Silver had an atomic weight of 107.880 though he had never tried such a combination, Mark attempted it now. To fail would mean the failure of his entire plan. There might never be another chance. If he failed, another minute would probably find him so full of bullets they'd have to bury him with a crane.

Ira's face took on an ashy hue, as he realized that he was trapped. There was no explanation to account for the gold's failure to cause a squeal. He also remembered Nona's brooch. And having nothing to say, Ira wisely said nothing.

Vargo looked leisurely about the room. His eyes roved over the faces of those beyond the glass which separated the studio from the anteroom. He motioned to two of his men. They placed themselves, guns drawn, at the door which led into the factory proper.

All the performers were now trapped in the two rooms. Not even a window offered any means of escape.

Vargo frowned momentarily as he raised hand to his helmet. The thing was becoming uncomfortably warm. But he lowered the hand without touching it. He studied intently the faces of those in the other room.

He raised the hand again, and scratched his scalp through the helmet, apparently musing and turning over a course of action in his mind.

"Of course," he said slowly, "I can just shoot all of you. That would be easier than penetrating a disguise, and it would be certain to get the right one."

He paused and frowned again. "But I'd much rather get my hands on this Mark, self-styled Protector of the Planet. I've a few tortures in mind for him. Suppose one of you tell me which is he. I'll let that one go free."

A number of emotions showed on the faces of the performers, but none offered to speak. Vargo frowned and moved the helmet about on his head, without loosening the collar. The thing was getting infernally hot.

Abruptly Vargo's face showed fear. He strode to the nearest of the soldiers.

"Loosen your helmet," he ordered. "When I take mine off, place yours instantly on my head. Ready now—don't leave my head uncovered an instant!"

The man did as ordered. He loosened the collar to his helmet and paused, both hands grasping his helmet, waiting for Vargo to remove his. Vargo did, with a lightning move which was made even speedier by reason of the fact that his fingers were being scorched.

The man instantly slammed his own helmet on Vargo's head. A tendril of smoke rose from the cloth of the one Vargo was forced to drop on the floor.

BUT THE great Vargo had let panic dim the processes of his brilliant brain. He forgot something. And forgetting it was fatal. For the instant the soldier removed his helmet, he fell under the spell of Mark's hypnotic wave.

With almost the same move that he had slammed the helmet

on Vargo's head, he snatched it off again, casting it to the floor besides the other.

Five shots rang out. Vargo's other soldiers had been trained to instantaneous action when anything threatened their ruler. The soldier dropped to the floor, bleeding profusely.

Vargo made no attempt to retrieve the helmet. Instead he turned slowly to face the cabinet, his eyes becoming glassy as he did so. For a minute he stood silently, while his soldiers wondered but feared to open their mouths.

Then he turned away from the cabinet and told them all to remove their helmets. They did, and immediately became motionless, rigidly staring at nothing.

The door of the cabinet opened and Mark stepped forth, his face haggard with the effort of his concentration. In his hand was a sheaf of paper which he gave to Vargo.

"You may announce Vargo, King of Detroit," he said wearily.

Ira, weak with the reaction of being snatched from a sentence of death, smiled sickishly and approached the microphone. But his voice was strong and assured as he announced the benevolent ruler, Vargo.

BACK AT headquarters was a scene of jubilant triumph. Plans for the future were being made, and for the first time carrying a degree of certainty with them. Fear of the Vocation Board was gone. Each man could go back to his work without being forced to face that body and account for his time while he had been gone.

Many of them didn't intend to return to their original jobs. There were other forms of endeavor more attractive.

The two men who had appeared as a comedy team had decided that they possessed talent as radio broadcasters. And Ira, temporarily, intended to head a company engaged in the manufacture of receivers.

Tolon and Gladys refused to make any plans. They had placed themselves at Mark's disposal, to help in the solving of the many problems incident to the reorganization of Detroit's industrial life. Beyond that they wouldn't go. There were too many years to plan for.

"But I can't understand," said Ira, "why you intend to leave Vargo as King of Detroit. Why not elect a new king?"

Mark shook his head. "As long as Vargo lives, he will rule Detroit," he said. "It lies within his power to direct the thoughts of those he has hypnotized. And he'll now devote himself to undoing the wrongs he has committed. The task would be impossible for a new ruler. I'd have to do it myself, and that would be too confining.

"By the time he dies, the younger generation will be grown up and there will be no need of him. As time goes on there will be fewer and fewer people who have been under his influence. They will all die eventually.

"But before they die, and before Vargo dies, their thoughts and ideals must be governed so that they will be happy without spending all their time and energy working in factories. Even though still slightly under the influence of hypnosis, they can be directed in such a way that their lives will be normal."

"How about the Vocation Board?" asked Ira.

"It's a good idea, leaving hypnosis out of it," Mark contended. "As a body of experts, concerned solely with finding the special aptitudes of young people just out of school, it will be a valuable aid to society. Its decisions don't have to be final—merely directive. Any one applicant will probably find that he has aptitudes along several lines. The final choice of his subsequent training will lie with him."

The large meeting room of the thieves' fraternity had been turned into a banquet hall for the celebration. Rugs had been removed for a space for dancing. A small orchestra, composed entirely of members, furnished the music.

It was while Mark was leading Nona in a waltz that Omega appeared. He did it quite suddenly, at Mark's elbow. His wrinkled countenance was the familiar one of the superannuated, but agile old man. He leered pleasantly.

"May I cut in?" he inquired.

Mark relinquished, Nona, and went back to the table where Ira, Tolon, and Gladys waited, eyes wide at the appearance of the old man. They had been watching Mark and Nona dance, and had all seen Omega suddenly take form.

"That's—" began Ira.

"That's him," finished Mark, as grim as he was ungrammatic. "Get Jan Thomas. We'll have to face this sooner or later."

IRA, FACE as inscrutable as ever, left to find Jan Thomas. Tolon and Gladys seemed to catch the tension in Mark's mind and were silent until Ira returned, bringing the bio-chemist with him.

"He seems like a nice old man," ventured Gladys.

"Doesn't mean a thing," said Mark. "He might just as well look like a spider, or a saint. He puts bodies on and takes them off like changes of clothes.

"Not that he isn't a fine character. Don't misunderstand me. He's finer than any human could possibly be. But he just doesn't see things the way we do. His viewpoint is something we can't begin to understand.

"There's no telling what to expect. He might be cosmically offended at what I've done. Then again he might pat me on the back for having spunk enough to defy him, and give you all his blessings. I wish I knew."

The dance ended, Nona brought Omega over to the table. Mark gravely introduced him to the others. He seemed very cordial. His eyes twinkled merrily, albeit they were a bit crossed at times. He perked up at the introduction of Jan Thomas.

"One of the Ancestors, eh?" he observed to Mark. "Then you've licked Vargo?"

"Thoroughly," said Mark, and explained the present situation. "… But there's something else I'd like to tell you about. Er… Suppose we adjourn to another room. Too much noise here."

It was getting a bit noisy, what with the free flow of wines and other beverages, but that wasn't Mark's reason for wanting to seek the privacy of another room. He preferred not to have too many witnesses when he sprang the news to Omega. And that turned out to be admirable foresight.

"You like it here now?" inquired Omega, as they left the room.

Mark nodded. "And so does Nona," he said. "We're going to bring both the children here."

"Both!" Omega exploded, as the door closed behind them, shutting off the noise of the revelry.

"Yes. Both," said Mark. "I've decided on another plan. Neither Nona nor I liked the first one."

Omega's face darkened angrily. He overdid it, though. It continued to darken, until he resembled a Senegalese even to the thick lips and broad nose. Gladys let out a stifled shriek, and he abruptly changed back. He smiled disarmingly at her.

"What an actor I'd have made," he said. "What's your new plan, son? It had better be good!"

For answer Mark took Tolon's arm and laid it beside Gladys'. Then he drew a knife across both. A streak of blue blood followed the knife, but the wounds immediately closed and healed.

CHAPTER XXV

NO HAREM FOR NONA

"SO!" SAID OMEGA explosively, "You've usurped my prerogative! You think you can judge as well as Omega, eh? How do you know these people won't beget idiots, criminals, or the like?

"No offense, Toots," he added to Gladys. "I could get idiotical about you myself." But he scowled ferociously at Mark as he said it.

"It wasn't really your prerogative," Mark reminded gently. "My blood was an accident. And I haven't done anything to—"

"There won't be any idiots or criminals!" interrupted Nona. "These two have proven themselves to be intelligent and good. As much so as Mark or I."

Omega regarded her thoughtfully. "You too, eh?" he said. "Didn't you know that I investigated your ancestors for several generations back before I made up my mind? What do you know about these two? There might be a vicious strain that'll crop up in the next generation. Meddlers! I ought never to have noticed you!"

He pushed his chair back and stood up. The chair vanished in a puff of dust as he kicked it aside to pace angrily back and forth across the floor.

He stopped suddenly, looking at Ira and Jan Thomas, who were keeping a discreet silence. "Those too?" he asked.

Mark nodded and started to speak, but Omega silenced him with, a gesture and resumed his pacing. There was a carpet on the floor and he almost wore a groove in it before he finally stopped. Mark and the others were nearing an advanced state of nervous prostration by that time.

"There's no sense in punishing them," Omega said, looking at the four who had received the injection. "It wasn't their fault. And it's too late to do anything about it. But you two—"

He fixed a baleful eye on Mark and Nona, who calmly gazed back at him. "You two shall suffer! All of you face the other wall!

They did. In fact they were afraid not to—although Mark was heeding a rebellious section of his mind, which insisted upon telling him that there was nothing to fear. He fought down his imagination, refusing to picture Omega's possible revenge.

Nona, however, was frankly apprehensive. She shivered a little as she faced the wall.

"Now," said Omega. "Mark. You back up about three steps."

Mark did so, and realized that there were more people in the room than there had been a moment before. To the right of him were two men, and to the left two more. His eyes widened in surprise.

"All right," said Omega. "You can all turn around."

They obliged, then gasped in unison. Five Marks met their startled eyes: all identically similar, down to the last detail. Omega had apparently vanished.

"They're spurious," said the middle Mark, stepping forward a pace and facing the others.

"Who's spurious?" said Mark of the left end. "Nona! You know me don't you?"

A clamor came from the others at this turn of affairs. They all turned to Nona and held their arms appealingly to her, beseeching her recognition. Then they fell to glaring at each other and muttering dire threats. Nona, pale and worried, looked from one to the other in indecision.

"Take it easy, boys," came a voice from out of the air over their heads. "We'll leave it to Nona to decide. That'll be a fine punishment for both of you. When she decides which is the real one, I'll destroy the others. Tough if she makes a mistake, eh Mark?"

ALL FIVE Marks nodded thoughtfully, then glared at each other once more. Nona weakly sat down, looking appealingly at the others. But none of them had a suggestion to offer. Each of the five looked like the Mark they had known since his arrival on their horizon.

"Ask them questions," Jan Thomas finally said. "Things which only Mark can answer. We'll leave the room if you'd rather."

"Won't work," said Omega. "Each of them is complete with all Mark's memories. They're identical in all respects but one."

Nona came alert. "What is that?"

Omega chuckled eerily. His disembodied voice gave them all the shivers, it seemed to be enjoying itself so thoroughly.

"The phonies know they're phony," Omega said. "But that won't help you. They want to keep on living, so they won't give themselves away."

Nona buried her head in her hands. A muffled sob escaped her. Five solicitous Marks stepped forward to console her. That almost resulted in a fist fight, but inasmuch as each knew that the others couldn't be easily harmed, the thing fizzled among a host of angry looks and gargantuan cuss words.

The air turned an azure hue for a few seconds—though that was probably one of Omega's little jokes.

Nona finally stifled her sobs—and came erect. She held her head defiantly. "I won't choose!" she said. "After all, I've had a lot of fun with one Mark. I should have five times as much with five Marks. That's final!"

Astonishment covered the faces of the five. Then four of them smiled and one looked angry. Nona triumphantly stepped forward and kissed the expression off his face. The others disappeared with an impressive clap of thunder.

"Smart girl," applauded Omega, resuming the shape of the old man. "I had you going for a few minutes though. And was Mark scared!"

"I wasn't, you old fraud," Mark claimed. "You gave yourself away when you said that nothing could be done about the blue blood of my friends here. You could change it back if you wished. I knew you were only fooling from that minute on."

OMEGA LAUGHED, the parchment-like skin of his sides crackling as he heaved. Omega was thorough when it came to sound effects.

"All right, all right," said Mark, "I was a little scared for a minute."

"I kind of thought you were," Omega chuckled. "But in regard to these four friends of yours. They're all right. In fact it might interest you to know that I had something to do with the quick development of that serum. Thomas will tell you that never before did his mind work so clearly as when he threw together that last batch of serum—the one that didn't kill the guinea pig."

Jan Thomas' eyes widened. "I thought—" he started. Then he nodded vigorously, not trusting his voice.

Omega beamed. "You know, Mark," he continued, "I believe in letting people solve their own problems, though I don't mind helping them a bit when they're on the right track. I was getting impatient there a few months ago when you kept putting off a decision on this matter.

"Naturally you didn't want this family mating. Neither did I. But you didn't seem to be doing anything in the way of following the only other course open to you. I had to get you started. Don't mind, do you?"

LATER, WHEN the celebration broke up and everybody, went to his own room, Mark looked at Nona quizzically as she prepared for bed.

"What's on your mind, if any?" she asked.

"I'm just wondering how good an actress you are," he answered. "You were certainly convincing when you intimated that five husbands would be better than one."